For the Flint Public Library

The Bed Time Story Book

Mark Binder

Mark Binder

Light Publications

Cover illustration by Rory Stapleton
Back cover and black and white images © 2008 Jupiterimages Corporation

Edited by Beth Hellman
Design consultation by Claudia Summer
Marketing consultation by John Horton

Deep appreciation for all the teachers, students, librarians, parents and principals who have listened over the years. Special thanks to the people who have taught my children to read: Joan Abrames, Miss Eileen and Sue Martin. Thanks to Rob and Pam Liflander, to the folks at Adams Media Corporation.

This is a revised and edited edition of *The Everything Bedtime Story Book* by Mark Binder, released by Adams Media Corporation, 1999.
Original editor: Pam Liflander.

ISBN 978-0-9702642-5-1
Printed in the United States of America
10 9 8 7 6 5 4 3 2 1

Light Publications
PO Box 2462
Providence, RI 02906
U. S. A.
www.lightpublications.com

Have an excellent day!

Dedication

For Max, Harry, Francesca
Chris and Brian
and their children
to be named later

Contents

2

Introduction

The initial edition was dedicated "To Max and the players to be named later." Now I have a basketball team of young folk, and I hope that my stories will continue to amuse them and their children and (many years from now) grandchildren.

Almost all of these stories have been altered. Some are shorter, some are longer, and some of the language has been modernized. A few stories have been drastically rewritten in the name of fun.

We searched old woodcuts and illustrations to accompany the stories. Some of them are quite ancient, and others are more modern.

There was also the question of what to do when we discovered that in the original version of "Chicken Little", Foxy Loxy eats the hero and all the other animals. We kept the nice ending. Fortunately, most of the stories in this book already came with happy endings, but we have left intact a few important stories that don't end with the famous "and they lived happily ever after."

As a parent (or caregiver), you can pick and choose what you want to expose your child to. Storytelling is a flexible art. (See the essay at the end of this book to give you even more ideas.) Edit out parts that you don't like in the same way that you might fast forward past a scary segment of a videotape. Elaborate on other stories when the children beg for more.

Throughout the collection I'll also be offering history, hints and suggestions that will make your bed time storytelling more engaging and fun for everyone involved.

This storybook will give your boys and girls windows into the wide world of literature and story telling.

Oh, and don't forget to finish with the most important words in any bed time story...

"Good night."

— Mark Binder
    Pembroke Villa
    Providence, RI, USA
    2012

The Three Bears and Goldilocks

There are as many stories about Goldilocks and the three bears as there are storytellers. The ending in this one is a little bit happier than it is in some…

READER TIP: Youngsters love exaggeration and enthusiasm. In this story, Baby Bear's chair doesn't just break, it breaks into a million billion trillion pieces. You can keep going (gazillion etc.) or raise your voice enthusiastically. Also, when Goldilocks reads the magazine, feel free to personalize it—select the child's favorite magazine, or change the magazine to a book, television show or video game.

Once upon a time there were three bears, a mama bear, a papa bear, and a baby bear. These bears lived in a house in the woods, which is very unusual for bears.

One day Mama Bear was making porridge for breakfast, but the porridge was too hot. The bears decided to go for a walk.

While they were out, a little girl with long golden curls came to the door of their house, and knocked. Her name was Goldilocks. She knocked and knocked, but no one answered. Goldilocks was lost and tired and very hungry.

Finally, she opened the door and peeked inside. "Hello?" she said, but no one answered.

Something inside smelled delicious!

Goldilocks went into the dining room, where she found three bowls of porridge on the table.

She tasted Papa Bear's porridge, but it was too hot. She tasted Mama Bear's porridge, but it was too cold. She tasted Baby Bear's porridge, and it was just right! So, she ate it all up.

Then she decided to go into in the living room and read a magazine. First she sat in Papa Bear's chair, but it was too hard. Then she sat in Mama Bear's chair, but it was too soft. Finally, she sat in Baby Bear's chair, and it was just right! She started reading her magazine, and then the Baby Bear's chair broke—CRACK—into a million billion trillion pieces!

Goldilocks was very tired now, so she went upstairs to look for a bed to lie down in. First she tried Papa Bear's bed, but it was too hard. Then she lay in Mama Bear's bed, but it was too soft. Finally, she lay in Baby Bear's bed, and it was just right. She fell fast asleep.

A little while later, the three bears came home from their walk. They went into the dining room, and sat down to eat their breakfast.

"Somebody's been eating my porridge," said Papa Bear.

"Somebody's been eating my porridge," said Mama Bear.

"And somebody's been eating my porridge," said Baby Bear. "And they ate it all up. Boo hoo!"

The Bear family went into the living room to discuss what should be done.

"Somebody's been sitting in my chair," said Papa Bear.

"Somebody's been sitting in my chair," said Mama Bear.

"Somebody's been sitting in my chair, too," said Baby Bear. "And they broke it into a million billion trillion pieces. Boo hoo!"

By now the Bear family was quiet upset. They went upstairs to check the rest of the house.

"Somebody's been sleeping in my bed," said Papa Bear.

"Somebody's been sleeping in my bed," said Mama Bear.

"Somebody's been sleeping in my bed," said Baby Bear. "And there she is!"

"GROWL!" said all the bears.

Goldilocks woke up with a start, and the bears chased her all around the house, until everyone was quite exhausted.

Goldilocks explained that she was lost and hungry and that she was very very sorry. Baby Bear was still very upset.

Finally, they all came up with an answer. Goldilocks helped Papa Bear fix the chair. She helped Mama Bear cook more porridge. And she taught Baby Bear how to make the bed. Then Goldilocks washed up all the dishes, and the bears told her how to get home from the forest.

And they all lived happily ever after.

The End

The Three Little Pigs

READER TIP: Make a big deal of the huffing and puffing.

Once upon a time, there were three little pigs who lived near a forest. They liked to eat and play all day and sleep all night. Winter was coming soon, so they decided to build themselves some houses.

The first little pig built a house made out of straw. The second little pig built a house out of twigs. The third little pig built a house out of bricks.

One day, a hungry wolf wandered out of the forest, and came to the straw house. BANG BANG BANG! The wolf knocked on the door of the straw house.

"Who is it?" asked the little pig, who was inside.

"I'm a big bad wolf!"

"Go away!" said the little pig. "We don't want any wolves."

"Little pig, little pig, let me in," said the wolf.

"Not by the hair of my chinny chin chin," said the pig.

"Then I'll huff. And I'll puff. And I'll blow your house in."

"Go ahead," said the pig. "Give it a try."

The wolf huffed. And he puffed. And he blew.

The straw house blew apart into a million billion trillion pieces.

"Eeek!" said the first little pig, and he ran ran ran to the house made out of sticks.

"What's wrong?" said the second pig.

"There's a wolf coming!" panted the first pig. "Lock the door!"

Just then, there was a knock. BANG BANG BANG!

"Who is it?" said the two little pigs, who were inside.

"I'm a big bad wolf!"

"Go away," the pigs said. "There's nobody home."

"Little pigs, little pigs, let me in."

"Not by the hair of our chinny chin chins."

"Then I'll huff. And I'll puff. And I'll blow your house in."

"Go ahead," said the pigs. "Give it a try."

The wolf huffed. And he puffed. And he blew.

The house made of sticks blew apart into a million billion trillion pieces.

"Eeek!" said the first and the second little pig, and they both ran ran ran to the house made out of bricks.

"What's wrong?" said the third pig.

"There's a wolf coming!" panted the first pig.

"He's mean!" gasped the second pig.

"Lock the door!" they both shouted.

Just then, there was a knock. BANG BANG BANG BANG!

"Who is it?" said the three little pigs, who were inside.

"I'm a big bad wolf!"

"Go away," the pigs said. "We don't like big bad wolves."

"Little pigs, little pigs, let me in."

"Not by the hair of our chinny chin chins."

"Then I'll huff. And I'll puff. And I'll blow your house in."

"Go ahead," said the pigs. "Give it a try."

The wolf huffed. And he puffed. And he blew.

But nothing happened.

So he huffed. And he puffed. And he blew.

But still nothing happened.

At last the wolf realized that the house was too strong to blow down, so he looked for another way in. He spotted the chimney on the roof, smiled a wicked grin, and began climbing up the wall of the house.

The pigs, however, saw the wolf's tail swish by a window. They built a fire in the fireplace, and put a big kettle of water on to boil.

The wolf began to squeeze his way down the chimney. He was thinking about eating those three little pigs, when all of a sudden he put his foot in the kettle of boiling hot water and…

ZOOM!

He shot out of the chimney like a rocket. He flew over the woods, over the mountains and landed with a big SPLASH in a lake.

And the three little pigs lived together happily ever after, in the house made of bricks.

The End

The Gingerbread Man

Once upon a time there was a little old woman and a little old man who lived all alone in a little old house. They didn't have any children. So one day, the little old woman made a boy out of gingerbread.

His eyes were fine fat raisins, and his mouth was rose-colored sugar. He had a gay little cap of orange candy, and a chocolate jacket. She put him in the oven and shut the door.

"Now," she thought, "I shall have a little boy of my own."

When the timer went off, she opened the oven. Out jumped the little Gingerbread Boy, and away he ran, out the door and down the street!

The little old woman and the little old man ran after him as fast as they could, but he just laughed, and shouted, "Run! run! as fast as you can! You can't catch me, I'm the Gingerbread Man!"

The Gingerbread Boy ran on and on, until he came to a cow, by the roadside. "Stop, little Gingerbread Boy," said the cow, "I want to eat you."

The little Gingerbread Boy laughed, and said, "I have run away from a little old woman, and a little old man, and I can run away from you, I can!"

And, as the cow chased him, he looked over his shoulder and cried,

"Run! run! as fast as you can! You can't catch me, I'm the Gingerbread Man!"

A horse in a pastures said, "You look very good to eat."

But the little Gingerbread Boy laughed out loud. "Hee hee!" he said, "I have run away from a little old woman, a little old man, a cow, and I can run away from you, I can!"

And, as the horse chased him, he looked over his shoulder and cried, "Run! run! as fast as you can! You can't catch me, I'm the Gingerbread Man!"

Soon the little Gingerbread Boy came to a town. He smelled so good that every one in the town tried to pick him up. They said, "Don't run so fast, little Gingerbread Boy. You look very good to eat."

But the little Gingerbread Boy ran harder than ever, and as he ran he cried out, "I have run away from a little old woman, a little old man, a cow, a horse, and I can run away from you, I can!"

And then he ran right past every one in the town. He turned and shouted back to them, "Run! run! as fast as you can! You can't catch me, I'm the Gingerbread Man!"

By this time the little Gingerbread Boy was so proud that he didn't think anybody could catch him.

Soon he saw a fox coming across a field. The fox looked at him and began to run. But the little Gingerbread Boy shouted across to him, "You can't catch me!" The fox began to run faster, and the little Gingerbread Boy ran even faster, and as he ran he laughed, "I have run away from a little old woman, a little old man, a cow, a horse, an entire town, and I can run away from you, I can! Run! run! as fast as you can! You can't catch me, I'm the Gingerbread Man!"

"Why," said the fox, "I would not catch you if I could. I would not think of disturbing you."

Just then, the little Gingerbread Boy came to a river. He could not swim across, and he wanted to keep running away from the cow and the horse and all the people.

"Jump on my tail, and I will take you across," said the fox.

So the little Gingerbread Boy jumped on the fox's tail, and the fox swam into the river.

When they were a little way from shore, the fox turned his head, and said, "You are too heavy on my tail, little Gingerbread Boy, I fear I shall let you get wet. Jump on my back."

The little Gingerbread Boy jumped on his back.

A little farther out, the fox said, "I am afraid the water will cover you, there. Jump on my shoulder."

The little Gingerbread Boy jumped on the fox's shoulder.

In the middle of the stream the fox said, "Oh, dear! Little Gingerbread Boy, my shoulder is sinking; jump on my nose, and I can hold you out of water."

So the little Gingerbread Boy jumped on the fox's nose.

The minute the fox got on shore he threw back his head, and gave a snap!

"Dear me!" said the little Gingerbread Boy, "I am a quarter gone!" The next minute he said, "Why, I am half gone!" The next minute he said, "My goodness gracious, I am three quarters gone!"

And after that, the little Gingerbread Boy never said anything more at all.

The End

The Little Red Hen

READER TIP: This is a quick, fun story, especially if you add in noises for the barnyard animals. If your child has a favorite animal (perhaps a pig or a cat) feel free to substitute, but try to remember to use the same animals the next time.

The little Red Hen was in the farmyard with her chickens, when she found a grain of wheat.

"Who will help me plant this wheat?" she said.

"Not I," said the Goose.

"Not I," said the Duck.

"Not I," said the Cow.

"Not I" said the Horse.

"Then I will," said the little Red Hen, and she planted the grain of wheat.

When the wheat was ripe she said, "Who will help me harvest this wheat?"

"Not I," said the Goose.

"Not I," said the Duck.

"Not I," said the Cow.

"Not I" said the Horse.

"Then I will," said the little Red Hen, and she harvested the wheat.

"Now," said the little Red Hen, "who will help me take this wheat to the mill?"

"Not I," said the Goose.

"Not I," said the Duck.

"Not I," said the Cow.

"Not I" said the Horse.

"Then I will," said the little Red Hen, and she took the wheat to the mill.

When she brought the flour home she said, "Who will help me make some bread with this flour?"

"Not I," said the Goose.

"Not I," said the Duck.

"Not I," said the Cow.

"Not I" said the Horse.

"Then I will," said the little Red Hen

When the bread was baked, (it smelled so good, warm and fresh) the Little Red Hen said, "Who will help me eat this bread?"

"I will," said the Goose

"I will," said the Duck

"I will," said the Cow.

"I will," said the Horse.

"No, you won't," said the little Red Hen. "I shall eat it myself. Cluck! Cluck!" And she called her chickens to help her.

And they ate it all up. Yum.

THE END

I Have a Little Shadow

by Robert Louis Stevenson

I have a little shadow
*   that goes in and out with me*
And what can be the use of him
*   is more than I can see.*
He is very very like me
*   from the heels up to the head;*
And I see him jump before me,
*   when I jump into my bed.*

The funniest thing about him
*   is the way he likes to grow—*
Not at all like proper children,
*   which is always very slow.*
For he sometimes shoots up taller,
*   like an India-rubber ball,*
And he sometimes gets so little
*   that there's none of him at all.*

He hasn't got a notion
*   of how children ought to play.*

And can only make a fool of me
    in every sort of way.
He stays so close beside me,
    he's a coward you can see;
I'd think shame to stick to nursie
    as that shadow sticks to me.

One morning very early,
    before the sun was up
I rose and found the shining dew
    in every buttercup;
But my lazy little shadow,
    like an arrant sleepy-head
Had stayed at home behind me
    and was fast asleep in bed.

THE END

23

For want of a nail

For want of a nail, the shoe was lost:
For want of the shoe, the horse was lost;
For want of the horse, the rider was lost;
For want of the rider, the battle was lost;
For want of the battle, the kingdom was lost,
And all for the want of a nail.

The End

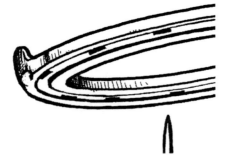

Three Little Kittens

The following classic Mother Goose poems are favorites of our family because their simple rhythms can lull children right to sleep. And they sound so sweet when the youngsters repeat them back to you! In this one, it's fun to take on the voices of the kittens and the mother cat: all children respond well to copying the animal noises.

Three little kittens,
They lost their mittens,
And they began to cry.
Oh, mother dear, we sadly fear
Our mittens we have lost.

What! lost your mittens,
You silly kittens!
Then you shall have no pie.
Mee-ow, mee-ow, mee-ow.
No, you shall have no pie.

The three little kittens,
They found their mittens,
And they began to cry.
Oh, mother dear, see here, see here,
Our mittens we have found.

Put on your mittens,
You happy kittens,
And you shall have some pie.
Purr-r, purr-r, purr-r
Oh, let us have some pie.

The three little kittens
Put on their mittens,
And soon ate up the pie.
Oh, mother dear, we greatly fear
Our mittens we have soiled.

What! Soiled your mittens,
You silly kittens!
Then they began to sigh.
Mee-ow, mee-ow, mee-ow.
Then they began to sigh.

The three little kittens,
They washed their mittens,
And hung them out to dry.
Oh, mother dear, do you not hear
Our mittens we have washed?

What! Washed your mittens,
Then you're good kittens!
Now it's time for bed, bye-bye.
Purr-r, Purr-r, Purr-r,
It's time for bed, bye-bye.

THE END

Sing a Royal Song

Sing a song of sixpence, a pocket full of rye;
Four and twenty blackbirds baked in a pie!

When the pie was opened, the birds, began to sing;
Wasn't that a dainty dish to set before the king?

The king was in his counting-house,
Counting out his money;
The queen was in the parlor, eating bread and honey.

The maid was in the garden, hanging out the clothes;
Along came a blackbird, and snapped off her nose!

THE END

Little Boy Blue

Little Boy Blue come blow your horn
The sheep's in the meadow,
The cow's in the corn.

Where is the boy who looks after the sheep?
He's under a hay stack
Fast asleep.

Will you wake him? No, not I.
For if I do,
He's sure to cry.

THE END

The Rain Poems

It's raining, it's pouring
The old man is snoring
Went to bed with a bump on his head
And he didn't get up in the morning

Rain rain, go away
Come again some other day
Little children want to play!

Three young rats with black felt hats,
Three young ducks with white straw flats,
Three young dogs with curling tails,
Three young cats with demi-veils,

Went out to walk with two young pigs
In satin vests and sorrel wigs.
But suddenly it began to rain
And so they all went home again.

THE END

Pussy Cat, Pussy Cat

Pussy cat, pussy cat
Where have you been?
I've been to London
To look at the Queen

Pussy cat, pussy cat
What did you there?
I frightened a little mouse
Under her chair.

THE END

Hey Diddle Diddle

Here are two versions…

Hey diddle diddle
The cat and the fiddle
The cow jumped over the moon
The little dog laughed to see such a sport
And the dish ran away with the spoon

Hey diddle diddle
The pussycat and the fiddle
The cow she jumped,
*   she jumped right over the moon*

The little dog laughed to see such a sport
And the dish ran away with the spoon

Yes the dish ran away with it
What can you say
But the dish ran away with the spoon.

THE END

The Little Boy
Who Cried "Wolf!"

O nce upon a time, in a village not far from here, lived a little shepherd-boy. Every morning he would take his flock into the hills to feed them grass and lead them to water.

Being a shepherd is rather ordinary work, and the boy often found himself bored. He would lie on his back and stare at the clouds, listening idly to the baa-ing of his sheep.

One day he got an idea. He would play a trick on the villagers. He thought the idea over in his mind once, twice, and then, yes, decided that it would be fun.

So, leaving his flock alone in the hills, he ran ran ran down from the hills into the village shouting out at the top of his lungs, "Wolf! Wolf! Woooolf! There is a wolf in the hills! It is eating my lambs!"

All the villagers who heard his calling immediately stopped working. They dropped their plows and tools, grabbed up sticks and stones, and ran as fast as they could out into the hills to help the poor boy.

But when they got there the wolf was nowhere to be seen.

"Where is the wolf?" the villagers asked.

The little boy could not answer, because he was laughing too hard.

Disgusted at this, the villagers turned on their heels and marched back to their work.

That was fun, the little boy thought. I must remember that.

A few days later, the little boy was again out in the hills, lying on his back, thinking about mischief.

The last time I tried that trick I had so much fun, he thought. Perhaps I should try it again. He thought the idea over once, twice, and then, yes, decided that it would be fun.

So, leaving his flock alone in the hills, he ran ran ran down from the hills into the village shouting out at the top of his lungs, "Wolf! Wolf! Woooolf! There is a wolf in the hills. It is eating my lambs!"

Once again, all the villagers who heard his calling immediately stopped working. They dropped their plows and tools, grabbed up sticks and stones, and ran as fast as they could out into the hills to help the poor boy.

"And where is the wolf this time?" the villagers asked.

But the little boy could not answer, because once again he was laughing too hard.

That was fun, the little boy thought. I must remember that trick.

A few days later, though, disaster struck. A wolf, a real live and very hungry wolf came loping over the top of the hill, and began killing the lambs.

In great fright, the boy ran for help. He ran ran ran down from the hills into the village shouting out at the top of his lungs, "Wolf! Wolf! Woooolf! There is a wolf in the hills! It is eating my lambs!"

The villagers heard him, but this time they didn't leave their work or pick up sticks or chase after him into the hills. They all thought it was another horrible trick. No one paid the least attention to his shouts, and when he came up and tugged at their sleeves, they turned away sadly.

When the shepherd boy finally returned to his sheep he found that they were gone, every single one.

It was a hard way to learn the lesson: if you lie to people, no one will believe you even if you are telling them the truth.

THE END

The Country Mouse and the City Mouse

Once upon a time, a Country Mouse invited her cousin from the city to visit. When the City Mouse arrived, he was shocked to find that the Country mouse had nothing for dinner but an old husk of corn.

"This is it?" said the City Mouse. "In the city we have food of all kinds! Come, let's go to the city and I will show you."

So off they went to the City Mouse's house.

First they stopped at the kitchen cupboard, where they nibbled their way into a huge bag of flour!

The Country Mouse tasted the flour, and thought, "Well, this is living indeed!" She was just thinking how lucky the City Mouse was when the kitchen door opened with a slam, and in came the cook to get some flour.

"Run!" squeaked the City Mouse. "It's the cook!"

Off they ran, scamper-skitter, into the mouse hole. The little Country Mouse was shaking and shivering with relief that they had escaped.

"That's nothing," said the City Mouse. "She'll go away soon, and we can get some more."

Sure enough, when the cook had gone and shut the door, the City Mouse took his cousin to the top shelf of the cupboard. There they found a huge box of raisins. They quickly gnawed their way into the box, and began pulling out raisins and eating them up.

This was incredible, thought the Country Mouse! Truly delicious.

But just then, there was a scratching at the door and a sharp, loud, meeow!

"What's that?" said the Country Mouse.

"Run!" squeaked the City Mouse. "It's the old Tom cat!"

Off they ran, scamper-skitter, into the mouse hole. The little Country Mouse was shaking and shivering with relief that they had escaped.

"That," panted the City Mouse, "was the old Tom cat. If he gets a hold of you, you are lost."

"I am never going to go into that cupboard again," said the Country Mouse.

"I know a better place," said the City Mouse. "Let's go down into the cellar. That's where they keep the really good stuff!"

Down they went into the cellar. It was truly an amazing place. On the walls were shelves lined with chunks of cheese. From the ceiling hung ropes of sausages, and on one table was an entire ham, smoked and waiting to be eaten!

It all smelled so wonderful that the Country Mouse had to try everything. She ran up and down the shelf, nibbling at cheese.

In once corner, she saw an extra rich and very delicious smelling piece of cheese on a strange looking table. She was just about to sink her teeth into it when her cousin saw her.

"Stop! No!" shouted the City Mouse. "That's a trap!"

"What is a trap?" asked the Country Mouse, skeptically.

"The minute you touch that cheese with your teeth, something from that table comes crashing down on your head, and you're dead."

"My goodness!" squeaked the Country Mouse. She looked at the cheese, and she looked at her cousin. "Please excuse me," she said, "I think I'll go home now. I'd rather have an old husk of corn to eat in peace and comfort, than have flour and raisins and cheese, but be frightened to death all the time!"

So, the little Country Mouse went back to her home in the fields, and there she stayed for the rest of her life.

The End

The Tortoise and the Hare

Over the hill and by the stream lived a Tortoise and a Hare. They were neighbors for a long long time, and every day the Hare rose with a laugh on his lips.

"Still asleep?" he called to the Tortoise. "You move so slowly, my friend."

When they were working in their gardens, the Hare would race around and have his planting finished before the Tortoise had even plucked his weeds.

"Still working?" the Hare called. "You move so slowly, my friend."

For many months, the Tortoise listened patiently to the Hare's taunts. Then, one day he decided enough was enough.

"Even though you're as quick as a politician's tongue," the Tortoise said, "I will beat you in a race."

"Impossible!" laughed the Hare. "I will bet you all my carrots that I will win."

"Agreed," said the Tortoise.

They asked their friend the Badger to lay out the ten mile racecourse and act as referee. It was a long run, from the stream, over the hill, around the great old oak tree, back over the hill, and then at last across the stream to the other side.

On the morning of the race, everyone in the forest rushed out to line the way and watch.

"On your mark," said the Badger. "Get set. Go!"

Away went the Hare, quick as lightning, and in a moment he was up over the hill and well on his way to the old oak tree.

The tortoise for his part had barely left the edge of the stream.

"Go! Go! Go!" shouted all the animals.

By now the Hare had reached the oak tree. Underneath the tree was a nice soft patch of moss. He looked back over his shoulder and saw that the Tortoise still hadn't even climbed the edge of the hill.

"It's time for a nap," said the Hare to himself. He lay down and was soon asleep.

The Tortoise never stopped and never paused. He went on, slowly to be sure, up the hill, down the hill and around the great old oak tree. He was just back at the top of the hill when the Hare suddenly awoke with a start.

"Where is that pesky Tortoise?" the Hare muttered.

And then he saw the Tortoise's tail just vanishing down the side of the hill.

The Hare ran and ran and ran as fast as he could, but before he reached the bottom of the hill, the Tortoise was already across the stream, munching on one of the Hare's yummy carrots.

Slow and steady wins the race.

THE END

Ten Little Monkeys

This is a favorite for youngsters. In one version we found, the Monkeys didn't "bump" their heads, but "broke" their heads. (And obviously they weren't sent back to bed.) That version teaches a firmer lesson, but also seems a little harsh in the way of punishment.

Ten little monkeys jumping on the bed
One fell off and bumped his head
Mama called the doctor and the doctor said,
"No more monkeys jumping on the bed!"

Nine little monkeys jumping on the bed
One fell off and bumped his head
Mama called the doctor and the doctor said,
"No more monkeys jumping on the bed!"

Eight little monkeys jumping on the bed
One fell off and bumped his head
Mama called the doctor and the doctor said,
"No more monkeys jumping on the bed!"

Seven little monkeys jumping on the bed

One fell off and bumped his head
Mama called the doctor and the doctor said,
"No more monkeys jumping on the bed!"

Six little monkeys jumping on the bed
One fell off and bumped his head
Mama called the doctor and the doctor said,
"No more monkeys jumping on the bed!"

Five little monkeys jumping on the bed
One fell off and bumped his head
Mama called the doctor and the doctor said,
"No more monkeys jumping on the bed!"

Four little monkeys jumping on the bed
One fell off and bumped his head
Mama called the doctor and the doctor said,
"No more monkeys jumping on the bed!"

Three little monkeys
    jumping on the bed
One fell off and
    bumped his head
Mama called the
    doctor and the
    doctor said,
"No more monkeys
    jumping on the
    bed!"

Two little monkeys jumping on the bed
One fell off and bumped his head
Mama called the doctor and the doctor said,
"No more monkeys jumping on the bed!"

One little monkey jumping on the bed
He fell off and bumped his head
Mama called the doctor and the doctor said,
"No more monkeys jumping on the bed!"

No little monkeys jumping on the bed
None fell off and bumped their heads
Mama called the doctor and the doctor said,
"Put those monkeys back in bed!"

THE END

Little Bunny Foo Foo

Little Bunny Foo Foo
Hoppin' through the forest,
Scoopin' up the field mice
And boppin' em on the head.

Down came the Good Fairy, and she said:
Little Bunny Foo Foo
I don't want to see you
Scoopin' up the field mice
And boppin' em on the head.
I'll give you three chances, and then poof!
I'll turn you into a goon.

The next day…
Little Bunny Foo Foo
Hoppin' through the forest,
Scoopin' up the field mice
And boppin' em on the head.

Down came the Good Fairy, and she said:
Little Bunny Foo Foo
I don't want to see you

Scoopin' up the field mice
And boppin' em on the head.
I'll give you two more chances, and then poof!
I'll turn you into a goon.

The next day…
Little Bunny Foo Foo
Hoppin' through the forest,
Scoopin' up the field mice
And boppin' em on the head.

Down came the Good Fairy, and she said:
Little Bunny Foo Foo
I don't want to see you
Scoopin' up the field mice
And boppin' em on the head.
I'll give you one more chance, and then poof!
I'll turn you into a goon.

The next day...
Little Bunny Foo Foo
Hoppin' through the forest,
Scoopin' up the field mice
And boppin' em on the head.

Down came the Good Fairy, and she said:
Little Bunny Foo Foo
I didn't want to see you
Scoopin' up the field mice
And boppin' em on the head.
I gave you three chances,
So now I'm gonna turn you into a GOON!
POOF!

And the moral of the story is:
Hare today, Goon tomorrow.

THE END

The Ants Go Marching

*These are **not** the official "Ants Go Marching In…" lyrics. There are so many variations that listing them all would take a fair sized book. If your family already has an Ants tradition, please change the words!*

The ants go marching one by one.
Hurrah! Hurrah!
The ants go marching one by one.
Hurrah! Hurrah!
The ants go marching one by one;
The little one stops to suck his thumb,
And they all go marching
Down into the ground
To get out of the rain.
Boom, Boom, Boom!

The ants go marching two by two.
Hurrah! Hurrah!
The ants go marching two by two.
Hurrah! Hurrah!
The ants go marching two by two;

The little one stops to
    tie his shoe,
And they all go
    marching
Down into the ground
To get out of the rain.
Boom, Boom, Boom!

The ants go marching three by three.
 Hurrah! Hurrah!
The ants go marching three by three.
 Hurrah! Hurrah!
The ants go marching three by three;
The little one stops to climb a tree,
And they all go marching
Down into the ground
To get out of the rain.
Boom, Boom, Boom!

The ants go marching four by four.
 Hurrah! Hurrah!
The ants go marching four by four.
 Hurrah! Hurrah!
The ants go marching four by four;
The little one stops to shut the door,
And they all go marching
Down into the ground
To get out of the rain.
Boom, Boom, Boom!

The ants go marching five by five.
 Hurrah! Hurrah!
The ants go marching five by five.
 Hurrah! Hurrah!
The ants go marching five by five;
The little one stops to give a high five,
And they all go marching
Down into the ground
To get out of the rain.
Boom, Boom, Boom!

The ants go marching six by six.
 Hurrah! Hurrah!
The ants go marching six by six.
 Hurrah! Hurrah!
The ants go marching six by six;
The little one stops to pick up sticks,
And they all go marching
Down into the ground
To get out of the rain.
Boom, Boom, Boom!

The ants go marching seven by seven.
 Hurrah! Hurrah!
The ants go marching seven by seven.
 Hurrah! Hurrah!
The ants go marching seven by seven;
The little one stops to look up at heaven,

And they all go marching
Down into the ground
To get out of the rain.
Boom, Boom, Boom!

The ants go marching eight by eight.
 Hurrah! Hurrah!
The ants go marching eight by eight.
Hurrah! Hurrah!
The ants go marching eight by eight;
The little one stops to shut the gate,
And they all go marching
Down into the ground
To get out of the rain.
Boom, Boom, Boom!

The ants go marching nine by nine.
 Hurrah! Hurrah!
The ants go marching nine by nine.
 Hurrah! Hurrah!
The ants go marching nine by nine;
The little one stops to straighten the line,
And they all go marching
Down into the ground
To get out of the rain.
Boom, Boom, Boom!

The ants go marching ten by ten.
 Hurrah! Hurrah!

The ants go marching ten by ten.
Hurrah! Hurrah!
The ants go marching ten by ten;
The little one stops to shout
"THE END!!"

The End

Ten Little Indians

This toe tickler is short and sweet, not politically correct, but great for a boy or a girl with the giggles.

One little, two little, three little Indians
Four little, five little, six little Indians
Seven little, eight little, nine little Indians
Ten little Indian boys and girls.

Ten little, nine little, eight little Indians
Seven little, six little, five little Indians
Four little, three little, two little Indians
One little Indian boy (or girl)

THE END

Diddle, Diddle, Dumpling

READER TIP: Change the name "John" to your child's name. If she's a girl, say, "Diddle, diddle, dumpling, my girl Sue…" If you have more than one child or the the name has too many syllables, either abbreviate, or cram them all in as quickly as possible. It might not rhyme, but it will still be more fun.

*Diddle, diddle, dumpling,
my son, John,
Went to bed
with his trousers on,*

*One shoe off
and one shoe on!
Diddle, diddle, dumpling,
my son, John!*

THE END

Wee Willie Winkie

(The original spoilsport)

Wee Willie Winkie
Runs through the town,
Upstairs and downstairs
In his nightgown.
Rapping at the windows,
Crying through the lock,
"Are the children all in bed?
For now it's eight o'clock."

THE END

Winken, Blinken and Nod

by Eugene Field

Winken, Blinken, and Nod one night
Sailed off in a wooden shoe,
Sailed off on a river of crystal light,
Into a sea of dew.

"Where are you going, and what do you wish?"
The old moon asked the three.
"We have come to fish for the herring fish
That live in the beautiful sea;
Nets of silver and gold have we!"
Said Winken,
Blinken,
And Nod.

The old moon laughed and sang a song,
As they rocked in the wooden shoe,
And the wind that sped them all night long
Ruffled the waves of dew.

The little stars were the herring fish
That lived in the beautiful sea.
"Now cast your nets wherever you wish—
Never afeard are we;"
So cried the stars to the fisherman three:
Winken,
Blinken,
And Nod.

All night long their nets they threw
To the stars in the twinkling foam—
Then down from the skies came the wooden shoe
Bringing the fisherman home;

'Twas all so pretty a sail it seemed
As if it could not be,
And some folks thought 'twas a dream they'd
    dreamed
Of sailing that beautiful sea—
But I shall name you the fishermen three:
Winken,
Blinken,
And Nod.

Winken and Blinken are two little eyes,
And Nod is a little head,
And the wooden shoes that sailed the skies
Is the wee one's trundle-bed.

So shut your eyes while mother sings
Of wonderful sights that be,
And you shall see the beautiful things
As you rock in the misty sea,
Where the old shoe rocked the fisherman three:
Winken,
Blinken,
And Nod.

THE END

I Know an Old Lady
Who Swallowed a Fly

I know an old lady who swallowed a fly.
I don't know why she swallowed the fly.
Perhaps she'll die.

I know an old lady who swallowed a spider
That wiggled and jiggled and tickled inside her.
She swallowed the spider to catch the fly.
I don't know why she swallowed the fly.
Perhaps she'll die.

I know an old lady who swallowed a bird.
How absurd to swallow a bird.
She swallowed the bird to catch the spider
That wiggled and jiggled and tickled inside her.
She swallowed the spider to catch the fly.
I don't know why she swallowed the fly.
Perhaps she'll die.

I know an old lady who swallowed a cat.
Think of that to swallow a cat!
She swallowed the cat to catch the bird,

She swallowed the bird to catch the spider
That wiggled and jiggled and tickled inside her.
She swallowed the spider to catch the fly.
I don't know why she swallowed the fly.
Perhaps she'll die.

I know an old lady who swallowed a dog.
Oh what a hog, to swallow a dog!
She swallowed the dog to catch the cat,
She swallowed the cat to catch the bird,
She swallowed the bird to catch the spider
That wiggled and jiggled and tickled inside her.
She swallowed the spider to catch the fly.
I don't know why she swallowed the fly.
Perhaps she'll die.

I know an old lady who
swallowed a goat.
She opened her throat,
and swallowed a goat!
She swallowed the goat to
catch the dog,
She swallowed the dog to
catch the cat,
She swallowed the cat to
catch the bird,
She swallowed the bird to
catch the spider

That wiggled and jiggled and tickled inside her.
She swallowed the spider to catch the fly.
I don't know why she swallowed the fly.
Perhaps she'll die.

I know an old lady who swallowed a cow.
I don't know how she swallowed a cow!
She swallowed the cow to catch the goat,
She swallowed the goat to catch the dog,
She swallowed the dog to catch the cat,
She swallowed the cat to catch the bird,
She swallowed the bird to catch the spider
That wiggled and jiggled and tickled inside her.
She swallowed the spider to catch the fly.
I don't know why she swallowed the fly.
Perhaps she'll die.

I know an old
lady who
swallowed a
horse.
She's dead, of
course!

THE END

This Old Man
(Knick Knack, Paddy Whack)

READER TIP: If you want, you can change the last verse "He played knick knack on my shin" to "Then he started all over again," be prepared for a long night.

This old man, he played one,
He played knick knack on my thumb,
With a…
Knick, knack, paddy whack,
Give the dog a bone;
This old man came rolling home.

This old man, he played two,
He played knick knack on my shoe,
With a…
Knick, knack, paddy whack,
Give the dog a bone;
This old man came rolling home.

This old man, he played three,
He played knick knack on my knee,

With a…
Knick, knack, paddy whack,
Give the dog a bone;
This old man came rolling hor.

This old man, he played four,
He played knick knack on my
    door,
With a…
Knick, knack, paddy whack,
Give the dog a bone;
This old man came rolling home.

This old man, he played five,
He played knick knack on my hive,
With a…
Knick, knack, paddy whack,
Give the dog a bone;
This old man came rolling home.

This old man, he played six,
He played knick knack on my sticks
With a…
Knick, knack, paddy whack,
Give the dog a bone;
This old man came rolling home.

This old man, he played seven,
He played knick knack on my hen,

With a…
Knick, knack, paddy whack,
Give the dog a bone;
This old man came rolling home.

This old man, he played eight,
He played knick knack on my gate,
With a…
Knick, knack, paddy whack,
Give the dog a bone;
This old man came rolling home.

This old man, he played nine,
He played knick knack on my spine,
With a…
Knick, knack, paddy whack,
Give the dog a bone;
This old man came rolling home.

This old man, he played ten,
He played knick knack on my shin,
With a…
Knick, knack, paddy whack,
Give the dog a bone;
This old man came rolling home.

THE END

Chicken Licken

One day, Chicken Licken was walking through the woods and plink! An acorn fell from a tall oak tree on her head.

"Oh my goodness!" said Chicken Licken. "The sky is falling! The sky is falling. I must go and tell the President."

So, Chicken Licken ran back down the road, and on the way she met Ducky Lucky.

"Chicken Licken, where are you going in such a hurry?" asked Ducky Lucky.

"I was walking in the forest and a piece of the sky fell on my head. I am going to tell the President."

"Oh my goodness," said Ducky Lucky. "The sky is falling! The sky is falling!"

The two of them ran into the farmyard where they found Goosey Loosey.

"Chicken Licken and Ducky Lucky, where are you going in such a hurry?" asked Goosey Loosey.

"I met Chicken Licken, who was walking in the forest," said Ducky Lucky, "when a piece of the sky fell on her head."

"We're going to tell the President," said Chicken Licken.

"Oh my goodness," said Goosey Loosey. "The sky is falling! The sky is falling!"

The three of them hurried into the garden where they saw Doggy Loggy.

"Where are you three going in such a hurry?" asked Doggy Loggy.

"I met Ducky Lucky who met Chicken Licken, who was walking in the forest," said Goosey Loosey.

"When a piece of sky fell on her head," added Ducky Lucky.

"And we are going to tell the President," said Chicken Licken.

"Oh my goodness," barked Doggy Loggy. "The sky is falling! The sky is falling. I will come with you."

The four of them hurried into the barn where they saw Horsey Lorsey.

"Where are the four of you going in such a hurry?" asked Horsey Lorsey.

"I met Goosey Loosey who met Ducky Lucky who met Chicken Licken, who was walking in the forest," said Doggy Loggy.

"When a piece of sky fell on her head," added Ducky Lucky.

"And we are going to tell the President," said Chicken Licken.

"Oh my goodness," barked Horsey Lorsey. "The sky is falling! The sky is falling. I will give you a ride."

So, Chicken Licken and Ducky Lucky and Goosey Loosey and Doggy Loggy all hopped on Horsey Lorsey's back, and off they rode toward the capital.

On the way, they met Turkey Lurkey.

"Where are you five going in such a hurry?" asked Turkey Lurkey.

"I met Doggy Loggy who met Goosey Loosey who met Ducky Lucky who met Chicken Licken, who was walking in the forest," said Horsey Lorsey.

"When a piece of sky fell on her head," added Ducky Lucky.

"And we are going to tell the President," said Chicken Licken.

"The sky is falling," said Horsey Lorsey.

"The sky is falling!" barked Doggy Loggy.

"The sky is falling," gobbled Turkey Lurkey. "Can I come along with you?"

"I will give you a ride," said Horsey Lorsey.

And off they all trotted toward the capital.

Now, it happened that as they were going, they met Foxy Loxy.

"Where are you six going in such a hurry?" asked Foxy Loxy.

Turkey Lurkey took a deep breath and said, "I met Horsey Lorsey who met Doggy Loggy who met Goosey Loosey who met Ducky Lucky who met Chicken Licken, who was walking in the forest."

"When a piece of sky fell on her head," added Ducky Lucky.

"And we are going to tell the President," said Chicken Licken.

"The sky is falling," said Horsey Lorsey.

"The sky is falling!" barked Doggy Loggy.

"Well, well, well," said the sly Foxy Loxy. "I think I can show you a shortcut."

So all the animals followed Foxy Loxy into the forest.

Now, Foxy Loxy planned on capturing all the animals and eating them up, but as soon as he tried to bite them, Doggy Loggy began to bark, Turkey Lurkey began to gobble, Goosey Loosey began to honk! Ducky Lucky began to quack, and Chicken Licken pecked Foxy Loxy right on the nose. Then Horsey Lorsey reared back, and they all rode away safe and sound back to the barnyard.

In the barnyard they met Kitten Litten. "Where are you six coming from in such a hurry?" asked Kitten Litten.

"Well," said Chicken Licken, "I was walking through the forest and I met Ducky Lucky who met Goosey Loosey who met Doggy Loggy who met Horsey Lorsey who met Turkey Lurkey, and then we all met Foxy Loxy and barely escaped with our lives.

"That's quite some adventure," said Kitten Litten.

"Yes it was," said Chicken Licken. "We were going to go somewhere, but we've quite forgotten where. So instead, I think we'll all go to sleep."

One by one all the animals fell asleep, and they never told the President that the sky was falling.

THE END

The Frog Prince

Once upon a time, there was a young Princess who loved to play with her golden ball. She loved to throw the ball high in the air, and catch it. Every day she would play in the garden with her ball.

One day, she decided to see how high she could throw the ball. She threw it up high, and caught it easily. Then she threw it even higher, and still it was easy to catch. At least, she threw the ball as high as she possibly could. It flew so high that she lost sight of it in the sun, and when it came down, she couldn't catch it.

Instead, the ball rolled away, and landed with a plop in the pond.

The Princess stood at the edge of the pond and peered in, but she could not see her golden ball anywhere.

"Excuse me, Princess," said a voice, "I can get your ball for you. Croak. Ribbit. Nee-deep!"

The Princess looked around and could not see anyone nearby, except for a small green ugly slimy frog.

"Did you say something to me?" the Princess asked the frog.

"Yes," answered the frog. "I said that I could get your ball for you. Croak. Ribbit. Nee-deep!"

"I'm not accustomed to talking with frogs," said the Princess haughtily. "Especially not the gross green slimy ugly kind."

"Well, then," burped the frog, "you shall never see your ball again." He turned to hop away.

"Wait, wait!" cried the Princess. "I'm sorry. Will you please get my ball for me?"

"Pretty please?" said the frog. "Croak. Ribbit. Nee-deep!"

"Pretty please," begged the Princess. "I am a Princess. I'll give you anything. All the flies you want, your very own lily pad."

"I already have all the flies I want, and my own lily pad," said the frog, "But I will ask you one small favor."

"Of course," said the Princess. "Only, please get my ball."

So the frog swam down into the pond, and in a few minutes came back with the ball.

"Ptui!" he said, dropping the ball at the Princess's feet. "Here is your ball. Croak. Ribbit. Nee-deep!"

She picked the ball up, and rubbed it in the grass, because it was kind of gross and slimy from the frog's mouth.

"Thank you, good frog," she said, and she turned to go back to her play.

"Wait," said the frog. "Aren't you forgetting your promise?"

"Oh, sure," said the Princess. "What do you want?"

"Nothing much," said the frog. "Only a single kiss from you. Croak. Ribbit. Nee-deep!"

"Kiss a frog?" said the Princess. "Eww, gross! You're green and ugly and slimy and gooey!" She shuddered and ran away.

That evening at dinner, the Princess sat with her golden ball at the table next to her father, the King.

"Your ball looks a little green today," said the King.

"Oh, that," said the Princess frowning. "It fell into the pond. I got it out, though."

The King nodded suspiciously. He knew how little his daughter liked to get her feet wet.

Just then, the butler came into the dining room.

"A frog to see you, your Majesty."

"A what?" said the King.

"A what?" said the Princess.

"A frog," sniffed the butler. "He says he has business with the Princess."

"Send him away," said the Princess.

"Bring him in," ordered the King.

A few minutes later, in hopped the frog.

"Oh, it's you," said the Princess. "I thought it was another frog."

"Do you know this frog?" said the King.

"I rescued your daughter's golden ball," said the frog. "But she has broken her promise to me."

"Is that true?" asked the King.

"He wanted me to kiss him," said the Princess. "Ick!"

"No daughter of mine will break her promise," said the King. "Do as you must."

"No, sire," said the frog. "I will not have her ordered to kiss me. She must do it willingly."

"Never!" shouted the Princess.

The frog sniffed and turned to go.

"Wait," said the King. "You seem like a nice enough frog. My child has need of a playmate. Would you like to stay with her, and share her meals and keep her company?"

"Daddy!" said the Princess, but the King silenced her protests with a look.

"I would be happy to share her company," said the frog politely, although he was a little dubious about it.

So for many many weeks, the frog and the Princess were together every waking hour of the day. They ate together, played together, and even rode horses together. (Well, the Princess rode the horse, and the frog sat on her shoulder.)

At the end of six months, as they were going up to bed, the Princess turned to the frog, and without really thinking said, "Good night, Frog." and gave him a little kiss on the top of his head.

There was a thunderclap and a lightening bolt, and the frog vanished in a puff of smoke.

Instead, standing before the Princess was a handsome young boy with gorgeous brown hair and beautiful blue eyes.

"Who are you?" said the Princess, stepping back. "What have you done with my frog?"

"I am your frog," said the man. "I am also a Prince. I was enchanted by a wicked fairy and turned into a frog. Only the kiss of a beautiful Princess could restore me."

"Well, why didn't you say so months ago?" asked the Princess. "I would have kissed you gladly."

"Because," said the Prince, "you had to do it of your own free will, without knowing the truth."

"I don't believe that you're really my frog," said the Princess. "Prove it."

"Hmm," thought the Prince. "Croak. Ribbit. Nee-deep!"

"Froggy!" exclaimed the Princess.

With that, the two embraced. They played together for many years, and became good friends.

Eventually they got married, and of course they lived happily ever after.

The End

The Shaggy Dog's Tail
(A Shaggy Dog Tale)

*READER TIP: As you will see, this story can go on forever—or until the little one drifts off to sleep. It is designed for days when your brain is offline. After the first few times, you can tell it without any thought whatsoever. If the child says, "No, tell me a different story!" then you can change it to a shaggy sheep or goat or squirrel, or whatever suits your fancy. This can be quite a fun game as long as you don't get annoyed. Hopefully, this **won't** become your child's favorite story.*

O nce upon a time there was a baby shaggy dog who didn't want to go to bed.

The baby shaggy dog pulled on the daddy shaggy dog's tail.

"Tell me a story," said the baby shaggy dog.

"Ok, said the daddy shaggy dog. "Let me think. Oh, I remember one…"

Once upon a time there was a baby shaggy dog who didn't want to go to bed.

The baby shaggy dog pulled on the daddy shaggy dog's tail.

"Tell me a story," said the baby shaggy dog.

"Ok, said the daddy shaggy dog. "Let me think. Oh, I remember one…"

Once upon a time there was a baby shaggy dog who didn't want to go to bed.

The baby shaggy dog pulled on the daddy shaggy dog's tail.

"Tell me a story," said the baby shaggy dog.

"Ok, said the daddy shaggy dog. "Let me think. Oh, I remember one…"

Once upon a time there was a baby shaggy dog who didn't want to go to bed.

The baby shaggy dog pulled on the daddy shaggy dog's tail.

"Tell me a story," said the baby shaggy dog.

"Ok, said the daddy shaggy dog. "Let me think. Oh, I remember one…"

Once upon a time there was a baby shaggy dog who didn't want to go to bed.

The baby shaggy dog pulled on the daddy shaggy dog's tail.

"Tell me a story," said the baby shaggy dog.

"Ok, said the daddy shaggy dog. "Let me think. Oh, I remember one…"

Once upon a time there was a baby shaggy dog who didn't want to go to bed.

The baby shaggy dog pulled on the daddy shaggy dog's tail.

"Tell me a story," said the baby shaggy dog.

"Ok, said the daddy shaggy dog. "Let me think. Oh, I remember one…"

THE END?

The Red Snowman

My family wrote this story together. We drew a picture of it first, and then made up the story between the three of us. You can make up stories too...

Once upon a time, on top of a little mountain was a big silver castle. Inside the big silver castle lived a red snowman. He was a very happy snowman, and loved to tend his garden.

One summer, the sun grew very hot, and the Red Snowman began to melt. He needed more snow, otherwise he would melt away into nothing.

So, he quickly left his castle, climbed down the small mountain, and climbed up a big mountain.

The top of the big mountain was covered with snow. It was cold and deep, and best of all it was red.

But, as the snowman stepped toward the snow, out jumped a gigantic purple lion.

"Roar!" said the purple Lion, "What do you want?"

"I just want some more snow," said the red snowman.

"More snow?" growled the lion. "Why do you need more snow?"

"So I don't melt away into nothing," said the red snowman.

"I see," said the Lion. "I will give you all the red snow you want, on one condition."

"What is that?" the snowman asked.

"You must travel into the great green forest," said the Lion. "Bring me whatever you find at the tallest tree in the forest."

The red snowman hurried down the mountain. He had never been in the great green forest, and didn't know what he would find at the tallest tree.

Finally, he stood at the foot of the tallest tree in the forest.

There he saw a blue mouse.

"Ah ha!" said the red snowman. He snatched the blue mouse up.

"Eeek!" squeaked the blue mouse. "What are you doing?"

"I am taking you to the purple lion, so that he will give me more snow."

"More snow?" said the mouse "Why do you need more snow?"

"So that I don't melt away into nothing," said the snowman.

"If you bring me to the purple lion, he will eat me up in one bite," said the blue mouse.

"I don't know what to do." The snowman felt sad. "All I want is to go back to my castle and work in my garden."

"I have an idea," said the mouse. "At the top of the tallest tree is a golden apple. You could give that to the lion."

"Then he would give me some snow," said the snowman. "But snowmen can't climb trees."

"Mice can!" said the mouse. "I will bring you the golden apple on one condition. Take me back to your castle and let me work in your garden."

The snowman agreed. The mouse raced to the top of the tree and plucked the golden apple.

Then, the two friends hurried out of the great green forest, and climbed the tall mountain.

"Roar!" said the purple lion when they reached the top. "What do you want?"

"I have traveled to the tallest tree in the great green forest," said the snowman. "I am bringing you what I found."

"The blue mouse!" said the lion, his teeth gleaming white. "I will eat him up in one bite."

"No!" squeaked the mouse.

"Not the mouse," said the snowman. "We have brought you a golden apple."

"I have always wanted a golden apple," said the purple lion. "You may have all the snow that you want."

"Thank you," said the red snowman.

"You're welcome," said the lion, politely.

The Red Snowman rolled and rolled around in the red snow, until he felt completely better.

Then he and the blue mouse traveled down the big mountain, and up the little mountain, until they reached the big silver castle.

"What a beautiful garden!" said the blue mouse.

"Welcome home," said the red snowman.

And together they lived happily ever after.

THE END

Little Red Riding Hood

READER TIP: By now, you know this is another fine story for playing around with voices. Children especially love it when the wolf pretends to be Grandma. Be careful not to strain your voice!

Once upon a time there lived a little girl named Little Red Riding Hood. She was called "Little Red Riding Hood" because she was little and always wore a red hood that her Grandmother had made for her.

Little Red Riding Hood was a very happy girl. She lived on one side of the great forest with her mother and father. Her Grandmother lived on the other side of the forest, and Red Riding Hood and her parents often visited her.

One day, Little Red Riding Hood's mother came up to her and said, "Little Red Riding Hood, your Grandmother is feeling poorly. I think we should make a basket of goodies for you to take to her."

"Sounds like a great idea," Little Red Riding Hood said.

So Little Red Riding Hood and her mother began to bake and cook. They baked chocolate chip cookies and a chocolate cake and a chocolate cream pie. Chocolate, if you haven't already guessed, was her Grandmother's absolute favorite. They also made her a big container of chicken soup so that she would feel better.

"Little Red Riding Hood," said Little Red Riding Hood's mother, "Why don't you go out and pick some flowers for your Grandmother. You know how much she likes flowers."

So, Little Red Riding Hood went outside and picked all kinds of beautiful flowers to take to her Grandmother. When she was finished, she came back inside and said, "I'm ready. Let's to go to Grandmother's house."

"I can't come with you today," said Little Red Riding Hood's mother. "I have to do some work around the house. But you're a big girl now, you can go through the woods by yourself. Just make sure that you stay on the path and don't talk with any strangers."

So, Little Red Riding Hood tied on her hood, picked up the basket and the pretty bouquet of flowers, and skipped off down the path to Grandmother's house.

Soon, she was deep in the forest, and she began to grow afraid. She had gone this way many many times with her mother and her father, but she had never walked the whole path to her Grandmother's house all by herself.

"I shouldn't be afraid," thought Little Red Riding Hood. "I'm a big girl now. I can take care of myself."

She began to sing, and as soon as she started to sing, she felt better.

But, not far from the path lived a wicked wolf. He heard the singing and thought, "Hmm, sounds like a little girl. I wonder if I can eat her for dinner."

The Wicked Wolf sneaked out of his lair and peered through the woods. There he saw Little Red Riding Hood skipping along the path, singing sweetly to the trees and the birds.

"Yes, indeed," the Wicked Wolf thought. "A yummy little girl. Hmm, I wonder where she's going."

The Wicked Wolf loped ahead and stepped out in front of Little Red Riding Hood.

"Hello there little girl," said the Wicked Wolf. "What is your name and where are you going?"

"My name is Little Red Riding Hood," said the young girl. "I'm going through the forest to visit my Grandmother. She's feeling poorly, so I'm bringing her this basket of goodies filled with chocolate chip cookies and a chocolate cake and a chocolate cream pie, and chicken soup to help her feel better."

"Sounds yummy," said the Wicked Wolf, licking his lips. He was feeling very hungry. "Can I walk along with you?"

The wolf, you see, didn't dare attack Little Red Riding Hood on the path, but he thought he might convince her to stray, and then he'd get her!

"No thank you," said Little Red Riding Hood politely. "My mother told me not to talk with strangers. Good day to you."

"And good day to you," said the Wicked Wolf. He made a great bow, and allowed Little Red Riding Hood to skip on past.

Now, the wolf had a plan. He waited until Little Red Riding Hood was well out of sight and then he ran for a shortcut that he knew through the forest. He ran all the way to Grandmother's house, and got there well ahead of Little Red Riding Hood.

He knocked on the door.

"Who is it?" Little Red Riding Hood's Grandmother asked.

The wolf coughed twice, and then cleared his throat. Then, in the sweetest voice he could possibly muster, the wolf said, "It is I, Little Red Riding Hood. I have brought you a basket of goodies, filled with chocolate chip cookies and a chocolate cake and a chocolate cream pie, and chicken soup to help you feel better."

"Mmm," said the old lady. "Chocolate is my favorite!"

She opened the door, and was quite surprised to see the Wicked Wolf standing on the steps, licking his lips.

Before Little Red Riding Hood's Grandmother even had a chance to scream, the hungry wicked wolf opened his mouth and swallowed her whole.

"Now," he said to himself, "let's see if I can get the little girl and the basket of goodies as well."

He put on Grandmother's nightshirt and nightcap, pulled down all the window shades, and crawled into the bed.

In a little while, there was a knock at the door.

The wolf coughed twice, and then cleared his throat. Then, in his best little old lady voice he said, "Who is it?"

"It is I, Little Red Riding Hood," came the young girl's voice. "I have brought you a basket of goodies, filled with chocolate chip cookies and a chocolate cake and a chocolate cream pie, and chicken soup to help you feel better."

"Mmm," said the Wicked Wolf. "Come in!"

Little Red Riding Hood opened the door and was surprised to find her Grandmother in bed and all the window shades pulled down.

"Grandma, are you very very sick?" Little Red Riding Hood asked. "I hope you're not too sick to eat the goodies I've brought you."

"Nonsense," said the Wolf in his old lady voice. "I'm very hungry. Come closer child."

"Why Grandma," said Little Red Riding Hood, "What big ears you have."

"The better to hear you with," said the Wolf.

"And Grandma," said Little Red Riding Hood, "What big eyes you have."

"The better to see you with," said the Wicked Wolf.

"But Grandma," said Little Red Riding Hood, "What a big nose you have."

"The better to smell you with, my sweet child. Come a little closer."

"Why Grandma," said the innocent Little Red Riding Hood, "What a big mouth you have, and what sharp pointy teeth."

"The better to eat you with!" cried the wolf. He leapt out of bed and ate little Red Riding Hood whole.

The wolf was so tired from all his eating that he immediately fell fast asleep.

Now, that would have been the end of Little Red Riding Hood and her Grandmother, except for a fortunate coincidence.

At just that moment, a brave hunter was walking past Grandmother's house, and he happened to wonder why the shades were drawn in the middle of the day. He had heard that there was a wicked wolf in the neighborhood and he wanted to warn the old lady to be careful.

The brave hunter knocked on the door, but there was no answer.

"Grandmother?" he said, opening the door just a crack. "Are you all right?"

When the light of the door fell on the wolf lying in the old woman's bed, wearing the old woman's bonnet and nightshirt, the hunter knew exactly what he had to do.

He dragged the wolf outside, killed him, and cut open his stomach.

There, inside, safe and sound, very much alive although very very frightened, he found Little Red Riding Hood and her Grandmother.

They cheered when they saw the Hunter, and felt very relieved when they saw the body of the dead wolf.

Then, after a quick bath, Little Red Riding Hood, her Grandmother, and the Brave Hunter sat down to a fine dinner of chocolate chip cookies, and chocolate cake, and chocolate cream pie, and chicken soup.

From then on, Little Red Riding Hood was very careful never to talk with strangers as she walked through the forest.

THE END

Puss in Boots

Many years ago, in a land far far from here, a miller had three sons. His eldest two sons were lazy and spendthrift. They preferred to spend their days lounging about the house while the third son helped their father in the fields.

One day, the miller died, and he left behind only three things. To the oldest son he left his mill. To the second son he left a donkey. But to the youngest son he left only a small black and white cat.

The eldest son sold the mill and went off to seek his fortune. The second son rode away on his donkey to seek his fortune.

The youngest son stared at the cat and said, "What am I ever going to do with a cat?"

The cat heard the youngest son's words, stood up on its hind paws and said, "Don't worry young master, I will take care of everything."

"A talking cat?" said the young boy. "I must be dreaming."

"Nonsense," said the cat, and to prove it he did a little jig. "If you will give me a cloth sack, a pair of boots and a nice cloak and a hat with a feather in it, I will bring you fame and fortune."

Well, thought the youngest son, what do I have to lose?

So the boy cut up an old a cloth sack, and stitched together a wonderful cloak, and a hat with a feather, and made the cat two tiny boots.

The cat put on the clothing, and danced about in joy.

"Now, don't worry," said the Puss in Boots, "I will be back in a while."

Off he went down the road.

In a short time, the cat caught a fat rabbit and popped it into his sack. Then off he ran to the castle of the King.

"What do you want?" said the guards.

"My master, the Marquis of Carabas has a gift for the King."

"Oh," said the guards, marveling at the strange cat. "Come right in."

The cat was escorted into the King's throne room. He bowed low.

"Sire, my master, the Marquis of Carabas would like to give you this fine fat rabbit."

"A rabbit," said the King. "Send your master my thanks."

"So I will," said the cat. "Until tomorrow." And then he bowed very low.

The next day, Puss In Boots caught half a dozen plump partridges and popped them into his bag.

When he arrived at the castle, he told the king, "Here is another present from my master, the Marquis of Carabas."

"Tasty quails," said the King. "Send your master my thanks."

"So I will," said the cat. "Until tomorrow." And then he bowed very low.

"This Marquis of Carabas is a very thoughtful man," said the Princess after the cat had gone.

Every day for the next two weeks, Puss in Boots visited the castle and brought a gift of one kind or another. One day it was a hawk, the next an owl, the day after that more rabbits and so on. Each day he gave the gifts to the king in the name of his master, the Marquis of Carabas.

Everyone in the palace had wonderful things to say about the Marquis of Carabas.

"He is very loyal to the king," said one. "A fantastic hunter," said another. "Where does he live?" asked a third. "I've never heard of him."

The Princess especially was curious about the thoughtful man who sent these gifts.

"What is your master like?" she asked the cat.

"He is young and handsome," replied the Puss. "And rich as well. Would you and the King like to meet him at his castle?"

"Of course," said the Princess.

"Of course," said the King.

"Then I will make the arrangements," said Puss in Boots.

The young miller's son was shocked when his cat returned home and told him that the King and the Princess would soon come and visit them.

"They'll see that I'm a poor miller's son," said the boy. "Then they'll know it was all a fraud."

"Leave everything to me," said the Puss. "My plan is masterful."

The next day the King and Princess rode forth from their castle in their carriage attended by their footmen and guards.

The cat saw them leave the palace and hurried on ahead.

"Quickly, master, quickly!" shouted the cat. "Take off your clothes and jump in the river."

"But I can't swim," said the young boy.

"Trust me," answered Puss in Boots. "All will be well."

Still, the youngster hesitated. At last, just before the King's carriage rounded the bend in the road, the cat shoved his master into the water.

SPLASH!

"Glub," said the young boy. "Glub!" His arms and legs flailed about.

"Help!" shouted the Puss. "My master, the Marquis of Carabas, is drowning."

When the King and Princess heard the cat, they sent their guards diving into the river to rescue the boy.

When they dragged him ashore, the Princess was embarrassed to see that he was wearing not a stitch of clothing.

"Thieves came and stole everything," said Puss in Boots.

The King ordered new clothes to be brought for the Marquis of Carabas.

"He is indeed a very handsome man," said the Princess to her father.

"You can not marry beneath your station," said the King, although if truth be told, he had taken an immediate liking to the bedraggled boy.

"My master is very very rich," said Puss in Boots. "He owns all this land, and our castle is not far up ahead. Come, follow me there."

Then Puss ran off so fast that the horses were hard put to keep up.

Every time Puss came across a peasant or shopkeeper he told them, "If anyone asks you who your master is, tell him 'The Marquis of Carabas.' Otherwise terrible things may happen."

Well, the Peasants saw no harm in humoring a talking cat, so as the King's carriage pulled past, they all told him that their master was the famous Marquis of Carabas

Now, the castle wasn't exactly empty. It was occupied by a gigantic and mean ogre. The ogre was more than just a giant monster. He was also a magician of great and terrible power.

"I'll outfox him," thought Puss, as he knocked on the gate.

"What do you want?" said the giant ogre, staring down at the tiny cat.

"My goodness, it can't possibly be true," said Puss in Boots, bowing low and removing his feathered hat.

"What can't be true?" asked the ogre.

"I heard from someone that you have magical powers."

"I do have magical powers," bellowed the ogre.

"I've heard that you can change yourself into a tiger or a bear," said the crafty cat.

"Of course I can change myself into a tiger or a bear," said the ogre. "Just watch."

The ogre said a magic spell and POOF, it turned itself first into a fierce white tiger, and then POOF, it turned into a ferocious black bear.

"But you couldn't possibly turn yourself into anything tiny," asked Puss.

"The tinier the better," growled the ogre.

"As tiny as a mouse?" asked Puss.

"Just watch," said the ogre. He said a magic spell and POOF, he turned himself into a tiny white mouse.

In an instant, Puss jumped on the mouse and ate him in one big bite. Delicious!

Then he ran to open the castle gates for the King's carriage.

With a great flourishing, Puss in Boots bowed low. "Welcome, your majesty to the home and castle of my master, the Marquis of Carabas!"

The boy, who was quite dumbfounded said not a word, which was fortunate, because dressed as he was in the King's finest robes, and standing as he was in the hallway of the great castle, he did indeed seem like a Marquis.

"This is quite a castle," said the King. "And you do have quite a bit of land. How, if I may ask, is your wife?"

"Alas," said the boy, finally catching on, "I am not yet married, but I would like to be."

The Princess blushed, and the boy blushed back.

They smiled at each other.

"Then it shall be so," exclaimed the King.

"You see, master," whispered Puss in Boots. "I told you that all would end well."

And that is how the Marquis of Carabas, who was once a miller's son came to be the Princess's husband, and later in his life the King of the entire land. And always at his side was his wisest and finest advisor, a small black and white cat who wore boots and a hat with a feather.

Together they all lived happily ever after.

THE END

Foolish Jack

After Hans Christian Andersen
There are many "Jack" tales. This is one of the siller.

In a land far far from here lived a merchant with three sons, Bob, Hank, and Jack. The two oldest, Bob and Hank, were known as the smartest lads in the whole county. They could add and subtract, multiply and divide, read and write. Now, Jack could do all those things, too, but he wasn't quite as quick as his brothers to brag about his accomplishments. In fact, he was known throughout the county as Foolish Jack, because he did nothing but lounge about all day, read piles and piles of books and look at the sky.

One day, word came that the King's daughter was looking for a husband. She declared a contest, that the smartest man in the entire country would be her husband. Whoever could talk sweetly and convince her that he was the brightest would be her Prince.

Well, Bob and Hank were excited by the challenge. They asked their father for horses to ride to the city, and Father gave them each a tall black horse. They packed books and plays and poems up in their saddlebags, because each one wanted to prove to the Princess that he was the smartest.

"Hi there," said Foolish Jack, "Where are you two going?"

"We are going to win the Princess's hearts with our fine words," said Bob.

"At least I am," said Hank.

"So you think," said Bob. "But I will prevail."

"Hey, I think I'll give it a try myself," said Foolish Jack.

"You?" laughed the two older brothers. "Why you're just a fool. You don't even have a horse to ride."

"No," said Foolish Jack, "but I have my old donkey. Wait for me. He'll do quite well."

Off rode the two brothers, laughing at their foolish brother's ideas.

Well, Foolish Jack wasn't much of one to hang about and sulk. He found an old saddle and put it on his old donkey. The donkey bucked and kicked, but when Foolish Jack hopped on, it took off like a shot.

"Yahoo!" Jack shouted. "This is some ride!"

Soon he passed his two brothers as if they were standing still.

A little later, Bob and Hank caught up with Foolish Jack.

"Hi, Foolish Jack," said Bob. "What have you there?"

"I've found a dead turkey in the road," said Foolish Jack.

"Ahh, a dead turkey," said Hank. "What will you do with it?"

"I will give it to the Princess and win her heart," said Jack. He put the dead turkey in his pack.

"What a fool," laughed the brothers, and off they rode.

A little while later, Jack's angry old donkey passed them at full tilt, and then a time after that, they found Jack again standing in the road.

"Hi, Foolish Jack," said Bob. "What have you there?"

"I've found an old pie plate in the road," said Foolish Jack.

"An old pie plate," said Hank. "It's battered and has a hole in the middle. What will you do with it?"

"I will give it to the Princess and win her heart," said Jack. He put the old pie plate in his pack.

"What a fool," laughed the brothers, and off they rode.

A little while later, Jack's angry old donkey passed them at full tilt, and then a time after that, they found Jack again standing in the road.

"Hi, Foolish Jack," said Bob. "What have you this time?"

"Look at this mud," said Foolish Jack. "It's so slippery and pretty."

"Mud," said Hank. "Think of that. What will you do with it?"

"I will give it to the Princess and win her heart," said Jack. He picked up a few handfuls of mud and put it into his pocket.

"What a fool," laughed the brothers, and off they rode.

At last the three brothers arrived at the city. There they found that more than two hundred men had arrived to show their intelligence to the beautiful princess. They were all given numbers and told to wait their turn.

While they waited, Hank and Bob studied their books and prepared their speeches.

While he waited, Foolish Jack watched the other contestants. Every single one of them rose, walked toward the princess, and bowed very low. Then, they looked up and saw the King's face frowning down at them. Then they turned and saw the television cameras and the newspaper reporters waiting to write down every word they said. Then the wisest and smartest and wittiest men in the entire country sputtered and stuttered and found themselves completely tongue-tied.

The King looked angry. Every so often he poked at the stove with a stick, and the fire flared up brightly. The Princess looked bored. Only the reporters seemed interested at so many young men making fools of themselves.

At last it was Bob's turn. He rose, walked toward the Princess, and bowed. Then he saw the King. Then he saw the reporters. Then his face turned bright red and he said, "Hot in here, isn't it?"

"Yes, it is," the Princess said.

"Hmm, hum," said Bob. And then he ran from the room in tears.

Next it was Hank's turn. Hank rose, walked toward the Princess, and bowed. Then he saw the King. Then he saw the reporters. Then his face turned bright red and Hank said, "It's really hot in here, isn't it?"

"Yes, it is," the Princess said, politely.

"Hmm, hum," said Hank. And then he too ran from the room in tears.

At last it was Foolish Jack's turn.

He rose, and walked toward the Princess. Along the way, he tripped, and he heard her giggle softly. Then he stood up and looked the King right in the eye. The King glared back, and Foolish Jack winked slyly. The Princess giggled again. Then Jack turned and looked at the reporters. He stuck his tongue out, and even the King smirked a little.

"Well, what have you to say?" the King asked at last.

"It sure is hot in here," Foolish Jack said.

"Yes, yes," said the Princess, the little hope she'd felt began to die.

"Would you mind if I cooked my dead turkey on the stove?" Foolish Jack said. He pulled the turkey from his pack.

"No," said the Princess, delighted. "You're welcome to, but we don't have any pots or pans handy."

"That's all right," said Foolish Jack. "I have this old pie plate." He brought out the old pie plate, held it up to his face, and winked through the hole at the Princess.

She smiled broadly. "What about sauce? You can't have a turkey without gravy."

"Hmm," said Foolish Jack. "I've got some gravy in my pockets." He reached into his pockets and began smearing the turkey with the mud.

By now the Princess was laughing quite merrily, as was the King.

"Aren't you afraid of the reporters?" asked the King. "They're writing down every word you say."

"Well," said Jack, "I've got enough gravy for them too."

And he threw handfuls of mud at the reporters and television crews until they all ran away.

The turkey went onto the stove, and cooked until it was quite tasty. That evening Foolish Jack and the Princess were married. And they lived happily ever after. Although I must admit that the reports from television and the newspapers were quite muddy on the details.

The End

I've Been Working On the Railroad

I've been working on the railroad
All the live-long day
I've been working on the railroad
Just to pass the time away
Can't you hear the whistle blowing,
"Rise up so early in the morn'"
Can't you hear the Captain shouting,
"Dinah blow your horn!"

Dinah won't you blow
Dinah won't you blow
Dinah won't you blow your hor-r-rn
Dinah won't you blow
Dinah won't you blow
Dinah won't you blow your horn

Someone's in the kitchen with Dinah
Someone's in the kitchen I know-oh-oh-oh
Someone's in the kitchen with Dinah
Strumming on the old banjo

Singing
Fee-Fie Fidle-i-oh
Fee-Fie Fidle-i-oh-oh-oh-oh
Fee-Fie Fidle-i-oh
Strumming on the old banjo
(Bum bum)

The End

She'll be Coming Round the Mountain

READER TIP: Have fun with hand movements to accompany the sounds. Pull the whistle, yank reins, wave, chop, rub, snore, and scratch.

*She'll be coming round the mountain when
    she comes (Toot toot!)
She'll be coming round the mountain when
    she comes (Toot toot!)
She'll be coming round the mountain
She'll be coming round the mountain
She'll be coming round the mountain
    when she comes. (Toot toot!)*

*She'll be driving six white horses when she comes
    (Whoa back!)
She'll be driving six white horses when she comes
    (Whoa back!)
She'll be driving six white horses
She'll be driving six white horses
She'll be driving six white horses when she comes
    (Whoa back! Toot toot!)*

And we'll all go out to meet her when she comes.
(Hi, Babe!)
Yes, we'll all go out to meet her when she comes.
(Hi, Babe!)
We'll all go out to meet her
We'll all go out to meet her
We'll all go out to meet her when she comes.
(Hi, Babe! Whoa back! Toot toot!)

We will kill the old red
* rooster when she comes*
* (Hack hack)*
We'll kill the old red
* rooster when she comes*
* (Hack hack)*
We'll kill the old red
* rooster*
We'll kill the old red We'll
* kill the old red rooster when she comes*
* (Hack hack. Hi, Babe! Whoa back! Toot toot!)*

And we'll all have chicken and dumplings when
* she comes. (Yum yum)*
Yes, we'll all have chicken and dumplings when
* she comes. (Yum yum)*
We'll all have chicken and dumplings
We'll all have chicken and dumplings
We'll all have chicken and dumplings
* when she comes.*

(Yum yum. Hack hack. Hi, Babe! Whoa back!
    Toot toot!)

She'll be wearing red pajamas when she comes
    (Scratch scratch)
She'll be wearing red pajamas when she comes
    (Scratch scratch)
She'll be wearing red pajamas
She'll be wearing red pajamas
She'll be wearing red pajamas when she comes
(Scratch Scratch. Yum yum. Hack hack. Hi, Babe!
    Whoa back! Toot toot!)

She'll have to sleep with grandma when she comes
    (Snore snore)
She'll have to sleep with grandma when she comes
    (Snore snore)
She'll have to sleep with grandma
She'll have to sleep with grandma
She'll have to sleep with grandma when she comes
    (Snore snore)
(Snore snore. Scratch scratch. Yum yum. Hack
    hack. Hi, Babe! Whoa back! Toot toot!)

THE END

The Ugly Duckling

After Hans Christian Andersen

Once upon a time in early spring, Mother Duck was waddling by the lake, when she found a strange looking egg.

"Hmm," said Mother Duck, "I must have misplaced one of my eggs."

So, using her wide bill, she pushed the egg back to her nest, where she sat on it and its five brothers and sister eggs for many many days.

At last, one by one the eggs began to hatch, and out popped six little ducklings. All the ducklings were cute and cuddly, all except for one. The one duckling who had popped out of the strange looking egg was the ugliest duckling Mother Duck had ever seen.

"What a strange-looking fellow you are," said Mother Duck. "Well, you're one of my babies, and I will love you very very much anyway."

The Ugly Duckling loved his Mother Duck and all his little brother and sister ducklings, and they loved him back.

But the other ducks on the pond were not very nice.

"What an ugly duckling," said one duck.

"He really isn't very pretty," said another.

"Ug-ly, ug-ly," teased a third.

The Ugly Duckling's brothers and sisters tried to protect him from the teasing, but it wasn't easy. Wherever they paddled on the pond, the other ducks would turn their tails, or laugh, or point, or call out "Ug-ly! Ug-ly!"

At last, the Ugly Duckling was so ashamed that he swam away from the pond, and hid himself away. He felt very lonely, and missed his mother and brothers and sisters, but it was still better to live alone than to be tormented and teased.

Summer passed and autumn came. The Ugly Duckling noticed some new birds swimming on the pond. They were much larger than ducks, and had long lovely white necks and beautiful thin beaks.

"How lovely they are," thought the Ugly Duckling. "But I am so ugly, I can't let them see me." So the Ugly Duckling stayed hidden in the rushes, and paddled by himself.

Then, one day, the Ugly Duckling heard a girl's voice say, "Hello, handsome."

He turned around and was surprised to see one of the beautiful white birds talking to him.

"Are you making fun of me?" asked the Ugly Duckling.

"Oh no," said the white bird. "I think you're very handsome."

The Ugly Duckling frowned. The lovely girl seemed to be telling the truth.

"What are you?" the Ugly Duckling asked.

"I am a swan, silly. Just like you. Only I'm a girl swan, and you're a boy swan."

"Me? A swan?" said the Ugly Duckling. "No. I'm just an ugly duckling."

"Nonsense," said the swan. "Come here."

The Ugly Duckling followed the swan into the middle of the pond, and looked down into the water at his reflection.

Many many months had passed, and the Ugly Duckling had grown into a beautiful swan!

He fell in love with the girl swan, and they were married. Imagine the surprise Mother Duck and all the Duck brothers and sisters felt when the Ugly Duckling came home with his beautiful bride.

"Why, you're quite grown up," said Mother Duck. "I always knew you were a fine boy."

And they all lived happily ever after.

THE END

Cinderella

O nce upon a time, a well-to-do merchant decided he wanted to remarry. His first wife had been lovely, intelligent, and kind, and had born him a lovely, intelligent and kind daughter named Cinderella. Unfortunately, Cinderella's mother died when the girl was quite young. Her father, the merchant came under the spell of the proudest and most arrogant woman in the city. A short time later they were married, and the woman (who was a widow herself) and her two daughters moved into the Merchant's house.

As soon as the wedding was over, Cinderella's new stepmother began to complain and nag. The house was too small, and dirty, and the girl, Cinderella was far too cheerful.

So, the stepmother put Cinderella to work. She gave her all the menial chores.

Cinderella had to do all the laundry, all the dishes, all the cleaning and scrubbing and mending and washing. Not only did she have to take care of her stepmother, but she was also responsible for every mess her stepsisters made. They took away her clothing and made her wear old rags. Still worse, the two stepsisters moved Cinderella out of her own bedroom, which had a lovely view of the garden, and made her sleep on a bed of straw up in the attic on the top floor of the house.

Poor Cinderella felt quite sad, sitting crouched on her bed, darning socks, while downstairs the three women drank hot tea and ate cakes. Still, she did not dare to tell her father, because his new wife already had the poor man terrified. All the stepmother had to do was to open her mouth and cough, and her husband was standing at her side, begging her pardon and asking what he might do next.

Despite all this hard work, hardship and heartache, and even in the ragged dress she was forced to wear, Cinderella was still more beautiful, kind and intelligent than her two stepsisters put together.

Now, it happened that the King decided to give a ball in honor of his son, the Prince. Invitations were sent out to all the best houses, and of course the Merchant's three daughters were all invited.

Immediately, the stepmother began purchasing gowns and linens and silks and shoes to dress up her daughters for their appearance before the prince.

"If you look well and act well," the stepmother advised, "then the Prince will fall in love, and our future will be assured."

Cinderella, of course, was put to work sewing the gowns, taking up the hems and letting out the waists. The dresses really were quite beautiful. The eldest sister's was made of red velvet from France, and the youngest wore a satin petticoat from Italy.

Cinderella helped them with their choices, and even braided their hair in beautiful plaits.

"Oh, Cinderella," teased the eldest, "wouldn't you like to come to the ball."

"Hush," taunted the younger stepsister. "You know that someone as dirty as she would never be admitted."

"Still," Cinderella agreed, "it would be lovely to see."

Both stepsisters looked at each other and laughed merrily at the thought of their dirty servant standing in rags at the ball.

At last the stepsisters were ready, and their carriage pulled up before the front door. Cinderella waved, and watched the carriage roll down the street until it was completely out of sight.

Then the poor girl burst into tears.

"Why are you crying, child?" said a voice.

"Who's there?" said Cinderella.

"I am," said the voice.

Cinderella looked down and saw standing on the table a tiny woman no larger than a teacup. "Who are you?" the teary-eyed girl asked.

"I am your fairy godmother," said the woman in a sparkly voice. "Why are you so sad?"

"I wish... I wish..." Cinderella began, but every time she tried to finish, her words were choked off by her tears.

"You wish you could go to the ball?" The Fairy Godmother finally asked.

"Yes," wept Cinderella. "But I am too poor and too ugly, and everyone would laugh."

"Nonsense," laughed the Fairy. "You are beautiful and kind and quite rich. I'll just give you a little help. Shall I?"

"Oh, please," Cinderella said.

"Run into the garden and bring me a pumpkin," said the Fairy.

Cinderella hurried to the garden, and brought back the biggest and finest pumpkin she could find.

The Fairy Godmother scooped out the insides, and then touched the pumpkin with her wand. Instantly it was transformed into a golden coach.

Then she sent Cinderella to the mousetrap for the six mice that were caught there, and with another wave the mice became six fine horses of a beautiful mouse-colored dapple grey. In the rat trap they found three rats that became two coachmen and one coach-driver with fine long beards and long white whiskers. Two lizards from the garden became two footman in green silk.

"Now," said the Fairy Godmother, "you have your carriage, we must see to your gown."

"I have nothing but this to wear," Cinderella said, and she began to cry.

"Oh, tush," said the Fairy. She touched Cinderella with her wand, and instantly the raggedy dress was transformed into a beautiful white gown of silk, with beads and pearls and diamonds glittering here and there. Even her slippers, which were worn and torn and dirty transformed into a pair of glass slippers, the most beautiful shoes the world has ever seen.

"Now, go to the ball," said the Fairy Godmother. "But be sure to leave before twelve o'clock midnight, because at the last stroke of midnight, the coach will be a pumpkin again, the horses will become mice, the coachmen rats, and the footmen will be lizards. And, of course, your gown will resume its old form."

Cinderella nodded eagerly, promised her Fairy Godmother that she would be home by midnight, and kissed the tiny woman softly on the top of the head.

"Now, hurry, child," said the Fairy.

The footmen opened the coach door, Cinderella hopped inside, and away they rode to the palace.

Now, the ball had been a little bit tiresome, but when the Prince heard that a beautiful Princess had arrived in a golden carriage drawn by six marvelous grey horses, he hurried out to greet her. He gave her his hand as she stepped from the coach, and led her into the great hall.

As soon as the two made their entrance, the assembly fell silent. The people stopped talking, and even the musicians ceased their playing. So beautiful a pair were the Prince and the strange girl that no one could say a word.

At last, at a signal from the Prince, the musicians picked up their instruments and began to play a waltz. He took Cinderella into his arms, and together they began to dance.

"What a fine dancer she is," said the stepmother, not recognizing the young girl.

"Her dress is more lovely than mine," complained the oldest stepsister.

"Her shoes are more lovely than mine," echoed the younger one.

"Quiet, you two," hissed the stepmother, as Cinderella and the Prince waltzed by. All three women smiled and waved at the Prince, but he had eyes only for Cinderella.

The hours passed like minutes. Cinderella danced and ate and talked with the Prince, and danced some more.

Then she heard the clock begin to sound the hour. She thought it was only eleven, but a glance at the clock's hands showed her that doom was near. Terrified that she might be discovered, she had time only to kiss the Prince softly on his cheek, and hurry from the Palace. She rushed down the steps, hopped into her coach, and was gone in an instant.

So quickly did Cinderella run away that one of her slippers fell off, and it was picked up by the

Prince who had turned to follow the girl whose name he hadn't even learned.

Just as they were out of sight from the palace, at the last stroke of midnight, the coach turned into a pumpkin. The rats and mice and lizards all returned to their original selves, quite confused I might add. Even though her clothing was once again rags, Cinderella did not feel sad. All that was left of her wonderful gown was the second glass slipper, which she put into her pocket. She remembered the warmth of the Prince's cheek against hers, walked all the way home, and went up to her attic bed of straw, quite happy and content.

The next morning, her stepsisters told her all about the ball, that the most beautiful princess had appeared and stolen the Prince's heart.

First, the Prince tried the slipper on all the other princesses and duchesses in the court, but none of their feet fit.

That afternoon, a proclamation was declared in the square that the Prince himself would be visiting every house in the city to find the owner of the missing glass slipper.

The two stepsisters knew that he would soon come to their house. They fluttered about all excited.

"Calm down," said the stepmother. "If the shoe fits, then surely he will make you his wife." The doorbell rang. "Open the door for the Prince."

"Welcome, your Highness," said the first stepsister. Her face turned as red as a mottled turnip.

"Hi," waved the second stepsister, giggling.

The Prince frowned, but asked the two girls to remove their shoes.

The stepsisters tried to make the shoe fit. They shoved and pried and pushed and squeezed, but it refused to take hold on their large and ugly feet.

At last, Cinderella peeked her head around a corner.

"May I try?" she asked meekly.

"You?" said the stepmother.

"That's just the cleaning girl," said the oldest stepsister.

"She's a nobody," said the second stepsister.

"Let her try," said the Prince.

Cinderella sat down in the chair and the Prince lifted the slipper to her foot.

It fit beautifully.

"Are you my Princess?" the Prince asked.

"I am," Cinderella whispered, shyly.

"She can't be!" said the stepmother.

"Impossible!" shouted the two stepsisters.

From her pocket, Cinderella pulled the second glass slipper, and slipped it onto her other foot.

Just then, her fairy godmother came in and touched her with her magic wand. In an instant, Cinderella was clothed in a gown even more beautiful than the one she had worn to the ball.

When they saw the transformation, her two sisters and stepmother threw themselves at her feet. "Please forgive us," they begged. "We had no idea."

"I forgive you," Cinderella said kindly. She hugged the three women to her, and some say that at that moment their wicked hearts melted and they became kind.

Then the Prince took Cinderella's hand, and led her off to the palace, where they were married in splendor, and lived happily ever after.

THE END

Jack and the Beanstalk

Many years ago, in the reign of Good King Alfred, lived a widow who had a young son named Jack. Jack was a nice enough boy, although he tended to be extravagant, careless and a little bit lazy. He didn't do a lick of work on the farm, and soon all the money was gone. All that was left was the old cow, Bossie, and even she had stopped producing milk.

One day, Jack's mother, with tears in her eyes said to Jack, "Son, we have nothing left but our old cow, Bossie. Take her into town and sell her that we may buy a bit of bread and some beans for our soup."

Jack, who had never been to town by himself, was eager to make the journey. He looped a rope around Bossie's neck and set off on his way.

At the crossroads half way to town, Jack met a man sitting off to the side of the road among the weeds.

"Hello, Jack," said the man.

"Hello, Sir," said Jack. "Why are you waiting so by the side of the road?"

"I've been waiting for you," said the fellow lazily. "You've got a cow to sell, don't you."

"Why, yes," said Jack. "Would you like to buy it?"

"How much?" said the fellow, without even standing.

"Five gold pieces," Jack replied boldly.

The man frowned. "I don't have that on me, but I do have something even better."

"Better than five gold pieces?" Jack said. "I'll have to see that."

Slowly the fellow stood up. He reached into his pocket and withdrew a small pouch. From the pouch he shook out four small multicolored beans.

"What are those?" Jack asked

"Magic beans," said the fellow. "They will bring you fame and great fortune. Shall we trade?"

Jack thought for a moment, and then agreed. He gave the man the rope, and patted Bossie good-bye. Then he put the beans in his pocket and lay down for a nap by the side of the road.

Just before sunset, Jack woke up with a start. "I'd better be heading home," he said. "Mother will be expecting me." And off he went.

When Jack arrived back at home, his mother greeted him eagerly.

"Well, Jack, I see you're back from the market," she said. "What did you get for our cow Bossie? One gold piece? Two?"

"Something even better than gold," Jack said.

"What could be better than gold?" said the poor woman, eagerly.

"Look," Jack said. He pulled out the pouch and spilled the beans on the kitchen table.

"Four beans?" his mother asked.

"They're magic beans," Jack said. "The man at the crossroads said so."

"Jack, you fool!" his mother cried. "You've been swindled by a demon. These beans are worthless. They'll hardly make a bite for dinner."

With that, the old lady picked up the beans and threw them out the kitchen window, where they landed in the garden.

Then both Jack and his mother went to bed without any supper.

That night it rained and thundered. Jack tossed and turned, barely able to sleep through the din.

The next morning, Jack woke and as was his custom, fetched the water bucket from the kitchen. He would fill the bucket with water from the well, and make a cup of tea for his mother.

Imagine his surprise when instead of finding the garden empty, he saw a wonderful woven beanstalk that was thick and strong and tall, reaching right up into the sky.

Jack looked up the beanstalk and realized that he felt a little dizzy.

"I'm going to climb the beanstalk," he told his mother.

The old woman tried to persuade her son to stay home, but Jack would not listen. At last, she gave him a kiss for luck. "Be careful, Jack," she said.

So, Jack climbed. He climbed and climbed and climbed. And then he climbed some more.

He climbed until his arms were tired and his legs could barely lift. Finally, he took a little rest. Far below he saw his house, and it looked like a little speck. "Well," said Jack to himself, "I've come all this way, it would be a shame to stop before I reach the top." Then he started climbing again.

At long last, he reached the top of the beanstalk, which just poked through a particularly dark cloud. Jack stuck his head up through the cloud, and was surprised to discover a beautiful field of grass. Way off in the distance, he saw a huge castle.

"This is very strange," said Jack. "Let's have a look." He jumped off the beanstalk onto the grass, and began walking to the castle. It took quite some time to get there, and by then he was very very hungry. (Remember, he hadn't had any dinner, breakfast, or lunch.)

At last Jack reached the gigantic castle. But how was he to get in? The door was as big as a mountain (or at least a very very high hill). Still, he knocked anyway, and soon the door opened.

"Who's there?" said a loud booming woman's voice.

"Just a hungry boy," Jack shouted back. He looked everywhere, but didn't see anyone, until he looked up and saw a giant's wife looking back down at him.

"You've very small for a boy," said the woman, "but I don't suppose you'll eat much. You can come in, but my husband will be home soon, and if he does you'll have to hide in the cupboard."

The giant's wife picked Jack up and carried him into the kitchen where she gave him a crumb of bread the size of a boulder and a morsel of cheese the size of a piano. Jack ate and ate until he was quite full.

Then he heard a distant rumble growing closer.

"My husband!" shouted the giantess. "Quick, into the cupboard."

The rumbles shook the house, and soon a gigantic giant burst into the kitchen. He had feet the size of horses, legs as tall as tree trunks, a head the size of a house, and two bloodshot eyes blinking in the middle of his particularly ugly face.

"Fee, Fi, Fo, Fum," roared the giant. "I smell the blood of an Englishman. Be he alive, or be he dead, I'll grind his bones to make my bread."

The giant began sniffing and snuffing, and looking in all the corners of the kitchen.

Well, Jack quivered and quaked, certain that the giant's wife would give him away and he'd be eaten by the giant.

Fortunately, just then, the giantess brought her husband his dinner, and so hungry was the giant that he quite forgot all about finding Jack.

When the giant had finished eating his dinner, he barked, "Wife, bring my golden hen!"

The giant's wife hurried from the kitchen, and was back in a minute with an normal-sized ordinary golden hen that looked surprisingly tiny in her hands.

"Hen, lay!" the giant ordered.

The hen clucked three times, and then sat down and laid a golden egg! The giant picked the

egg up, squinted at it, and then put the egg in his pocket. Then he fell asleep at the table, his beard dribbling into his soup.

Well, Jack saw his opportunity. He jumped from the cupboard onto the table and snatched up the golden hen. Then he ran as fast as he could out of the castle, across the great green field, and began climbing down the beanstalk.

It was nearly midnight by the time Jack returned home, and his mother was quite frantic.

"Jack," she said, "where have you been?"

"Winning riches," said the young boy. He reached into his shirt, and brought out the golden hen, which had fallen asleep while he had climbed down.

"A chicken for dinner!" cried his mother, snatching up a kitchen knife. "Good lad!"

"No!" Jack raised his hand. "Watch this. Hen, lay!"

And the hen clucked three times, and then sat down and laid a golden egg.

Jack plucked the egg from underneath the hen and showed it to his mother. She tapped it against a skillet, and was a little disappointed when it didn't crack and make a nice omelet. Then Jack pointed out that eggs made of solid gold would be much more valuable than the ordinary white or brown kind.

The two of them danced and talked until dawn. Then the old lady went into town and sold the golden egg for enough money to feed a family of fifty for a month. From that day on, Jack and his mother lived well and happily, taking the eggs that the golden hen laid and selling them for whatever they needed.

In ordinary circumstances, that would be the end of our story, but Jack was not an ordinary boy. Soon, he found his mind wandering back to the marvelous land high up in the sky.

One morning he called to his mother, "I'm going to climb the beanstalk."

The old woman tried to persuade her son to stay home, but Jack would not listen. At last, she gave him a kiss for luck. "Be careful, Jack," she said.

Jack climbed and climbed and climbed. And then he climbed some more. He climbed until his arms were tired and his legs could barely lift. This time, however, he didn't take a break until he had reached the very top and could see the field of tall green grass and the giant's castle off in the distance. When he'd recovered his breath, he ran across the field, and again knocked on the door.

Once again, the giant's wife opened the door and asked who was there.

"A hungry little boy," Jack said, smiling and waving.

"Go away," said the giant's wife. "The last time a little boy came, he stole away my husband's golden hen."

"But I've come such a long way," said Jack, "and I'm very hungry."

"Very well," the giantess said. Even though her husband was a man-eater, she had a soft spot in her heart for tiny boys. "I'll give you a quick bite, but if my husband comes home early, I'll have to hide you in the cupboard."

The giantess carried Jack into the kitchen and gave him some enormous crumbs of bread and cheese. Jack ate, and waited for the thunder in the distance that signaled the coming of the giant.

"My husband is coming!" said the giantess. "Quick, into the cupboard with you."

A moment later the kitchen door burst open and in came the giant.

"Fee, Fi, Fo, Fum," roared the giant. "I smell the blood of an Englishman. Be he alive, or be he dead, I'll grind his bones to make my bread."

The giant began sniffing and snuffing, and looking in all the corners of the kitchen.

Seeing the giant's immense size, and his fearsome face for a second time, Jack wondered if coming back to the castle was such a good idea. Still, it was too late to complain, and too early to run away.

Fortunately, the giant's wife once again distracted her husband with dinner. After the giant had eaten his fill, he ordered, "Wife, bring my harp."

The giant's wife scurried out, and then hurried back with a perfectly ordinary sized harp, which she set on the table in front of her husband.

"Harp, play!" the giant roared.

Immediately the tiny (for a giant) harp began playing the most beautiful tunes. It even sang accompaniment!

"Now that is something that I could make my name with," thought Jack. He waited until the giant had fallen asleep with his mustache in the gravy, and then he leaped from the cabinet onto the kitchen table.

He snatched up the harp and began to run.

This time, Jack's escape was not so simple. As soon as Jack touched the harp, it began to shout, "Master! Master! A thief! A thief!"

The giant woke with a roar, and Jack ran as fast as he could out of the giant's castle and across the great field. He didn't look back once. But, when reached the beanstalk, he saw that he was only a little bit a head of the giant. Jack jumped onto the beanstalk and began sliding down it as fast as he could for dear life.

The giant paused a moment, considered the strange bean plant, and then followed, climbing down slowly and carefully. (Giants, if you can believe it, are frequently afraid of heights.)

Meanwhile, Jack had reached the bottom of the beanstalk.

"Mother, mother, bring an ax!" Jack shouted.

"Oh, there you are," his mother said. "I was just beginning to…"

"An ax! Hurry!"

The old woman ran to the woodpile, while Jack caught his breath. She handed him the ax, and he began hacking away at the beanstalk.

Chop, chop, chop. By now they could just see the giant's feet high up in the sky. Chop Chop. Closer and closer.

And then, with a sudden "crack!" the beanstalk snapped and fell.

The giant fell headlong into the side of a hill and was instantly killed.

After that, things were quiet for quite some time. The giant's wife became the leader of the land in the sky, which grew rich and prosperous.

Jack himself became well known as a famous giant killer, and had many adventures with his magic harp. But from that day on, he was quite careful to make sure that his mother was well taken care of.

And they all lived happily ever after.

The End

It's Aloud
Reading and Sharing Stories With Young People

You don't have to work hard to help your child to read!

A concert pianist recently told my daughter that the secret of piano **wasn't** just practicing.

"It's playing. You have to play," he said. "If you only practice but never play, you'll learn your chops, but have no soul, no joy, and no motivation. If you play and play and play, then you challenge yourself and will practice in order to play even better."

Reading stories to children is play. That's why youngsters who have stories read with them learn how to read faster and earlier. They get the joy of the story without work or study. Then they realize that the letters spell words, and the words paint the story. The sentences tell what the characters say and do and think. It's like television, but you can take it at your own pace.

You can start at the beginning or in the middle or skip straight to the end without pushing any buttons. Your imagination fills in the blanks. And no commercials.

Here are some of my favorite tools for parents, teachers and caregivers of all abilities to play with.

When, how and what to read

• Start reading aloud and sharing stories with your kids now. It's never too early (or too late) to read aloud and tell stories. Babies love to look at pictures. High school students want to know what your life was like. (Especially the worst parts.) Most folk enjoy whoppers about how different it was "In the old days..."

• If you're telling stories with infants, almost any book will do. Babies love to literally eat up books. You could let them chew on the pages, but make sure they don't choke. Let the little ones get comfortable in your lap, turning the pages and looking at the pictures. As they turn the pages, you read the words. Over and over and

over again. You'll may find that your attention span is shorter than theirs. Pick books you like to read. Look for books with fun pictures, and fun language.

• Collect books. Get them new or used, at garage sales or surplus bins at libraries. Let books pile up, build book shelves. Give books as birthday presents. Trade with other families.

• Whatever book the child picks, read it. With children, familiarity breeds contentment. (If you really can't stand a book, give it away or recycle it.

Once that book is lost and out of the house, the child will forget and find a new favorite.)

• Lap reading is great. Children love the warmth, and after a long day at work you could use the snuggles. One day, sooner than you think, you'll be reading a book, sniffing your child's hair and smiling at a memory that will last forever.

• Don't try to be educational—unless the child expresses an interest in a particular subject. If you're always interrupting with "What color is that? What letter is that?" then storytelling and reading will become just another time for learning the rules of life.

• If setting a daily reading time helps, then do it. If not, then do whatever works. Kids love routines, but if you can't manage one (single caregiver families have a really rough time with this) than catch it when you can. After work. Before bed. After brushing teeth. Bring books to the beach. On the bus or airplane... Get creative.

• Keep reading, even with older kids. It gives them a chance to stop being cool for a while. Find chapter books and read them for a year. Make up stories yourself or do it together. Don't make them sit on your lap, but keep them close. They'll be gone soon enough.

• Skip parts you aren't comfortable with. Give Grimm's Fairy Tales happy endings.

How-to Tips

People say, "You're a writer. I bet your kids get the best stories." Well, of course they do... sometimes. And sometimes I'm just tired. So, like anyone else, I'll just grab whatever's nearest and shortest and plod along.

One day I was watching my mother read to my kids. She was awful. Flat voice, reading a little too fast. They didn't care. They loved the special time that she was taking to read to them. Besides, you'll improve—Mom's much better now.

That said, these storytelling tips can make the experience more fun both for you and the child.
• Use voices. High, low, gravely, cartoon, foreign accents. Whatever. Imitate people you know. Make noises and sound effects. Yes it's silly, that's the point. One hitch, with the littlest—if you use a sound in a story, be prepared to use it again and again...
• But don't use voices if the youngsters don't want you to. That's ok too.
• Change your pace. Sometimes read slowly, sometimes read fast. It's not a race. Let the rhythm

of the story help you out. Avoid making every sentence sound the same. Instead, have fun!

• Pronounce consonants. Hit those Ts and Ds and Ks. Find stories with lots of word play.

• If you're child's not done, repeat the same page or sentence.

• You look at the pictures too. Add words or lines if you want. Ask questions. (Sparingly.)

• Make the stories yours. Change character names to your child's names. Elaborate on descriptions. In Red Riding Hood, change the treats Red brings to Grandmother.

• When stories get old and boring to you, pretend to mess up. Instead of reading, "Good night mouse" read "Good night beaver." Your kids will correct you.

• Keep breathing. That seems obvious, but sound and breath are intimately linked. Reading time can be a meditation time for you and your family.

So relax, have fun, and read!

THE END!

About the Author

Mark Binder writes and tells stories for children, teens, families and adults.

He tours the United States sharing his stories and love of the written and spoken word with people of all ages. He has performed on stage and in classrooms, in festivals, community centers, churches, shuls and even in parking lots.

He is a frequent contributor to *Cricket Magazine,* and more than 60,000 copies of his *Bed Time Stories* are in print.

He is the author of the novel, *The Brothers Schlemiel,* and a collection of humorous "autobiographical" stories called, *It Ate My Sister.* His story collection, *A Hanukkah Present* was finalist and runner-up for the 2007 National Jewish Book Award for Family Literature.

Mark is also an award-winning recording artist. His first CD, *Classic Stories for Boys and Girls* won both an iParenting Media award and a Children's Music Web award. The audio edition of *A Chanukah Present* won a **Storytelling World Honor Award.**

He is the founder of the American Story Theater, and occasionally teaches a course at the Rhode Island School of Design called "Telling Lies."

Mark practices Aikido and lives in Providence, Rhode Island with his wife and children.

A Special Note of Thanks to our Readers

If you enjoyed this work, please look for more books, stories and recordings by Mark Binder. Softcover • eBook • Audio Download on Amazon, Kindle, Nook, Android, iPad and iTunes

Kings, Wolves, Princesses and Lions

The Bed Time Story Book, Volume 2. Grades 1-3 New and Classic Tales for Young Readers.

Genies, Giants and a Walrus

The Bed Time Story Book, Volume 3. Grades 3-5 Amazing Adventures and Terrific Tall Tales.

"Genies, Giants and a Walrus" includes some of the world's best adventure stories, selected and edited for the pleasure of voracious young readers. From Gilgamesh and the Arabian Nights to Norse Mythology and the American West, these are stories that both girls and boys will enjoy reading and rereading.

It Ate My Sister (and other family stories)

Includes, The PI Kid, Runninghead, Ellen vs. The Snakes, and more. "These stories are true," Mark Binder writes, "and some of them really happened." Ages 10 through adult with a sense of humor.

Stories for Peace

Ten stories plus three essays. Includes a new section on cyberbullying. All ages.

Classic Stories for Boys and Girls (audio)

An award-winning collection of favorite ten stories including "The Short Tale of Erika P. Spunk." "Jack and the Beanstalk" and more. Winner: Children's Music Web Award, iParenting Media Award. Ages 4-10.

Tall Tales, Whoppers and Lies (audio)

Recorded live at the New England Folk Festival on April 21, 2002 and April 26, 2003. Fun stories for all Ages.

It was a dark and stormy night... (audio)

Vampires... Corpses... Mangled Harry Potter... Eight Thrilling, Chilling and Humorous Halloween Stories. Ages 11 and up.

A Holiday Present (audio)

Christmas, Kwanzaa, Hanukkkah, Ramadan, Diwali, Solstice and New Year! Seven stories recorded at a live spoken-word concert. Warm, joyful and fun adventures celebrating giving and family. Ages 6 and family.

For a **free** bookmark, please send a
Self-Addressed Stamped Envelope to:
Bookmark
Light Publications
PO Box 2462
Providence, RI 02906

Have Mark Binder come to your school or speak at your next event

---

Mark Binder is available for author visits, book signings, story concerts, keynotes, workshops, full-day seminars and residencies. He captures the attention of all ages: PK, Elementary, Middle and High Schools, as well as multiple generations with family programs. All of Mark's presentations are a combination of education, entertainment and fun.

Mark uses humor, storytelling, movements, songs, and demonstrations to engage listeners of all ages.

He believes in the power of the written and spoken word to connect people and transmit joy.

For information about how to book Mark for your event, visit http://storyamonth.com/

CPSIA information can be obtained at www.ICGtesting.com
Printed in the USA
BVOW071654120612

292462BV00001B/24/P